Please check all items for damages
before leaving the Library.
Thereafter you will be held
responsible for all injuries
to items beyond reasonable wear.

HANS BAUER AND
CATHERINE MASCIOLA

WITH ILLUSTRATIONS BY CATHERINE MASCIOLA

AMAZON CHILDREN'S PUBLISHING

Y
FICTION
BAU

Text copyright © 2012 by Columbia Pictures Industries, Inc.
Art copyright © 2012 by Marshall Cavendish Corporation

Amazon Publishing
Attn: Amazon Children's Publishing
P.O. Box 400818
Las Vegas, NV 89149
www.amazon.com/amazonchildrenspublishing

Trademarks of the Catfish Institute are used by permission.

Library of Congress Cataloging-in-Publication Data

Bauer, Hans, 1951-
Fishtale / by Hans Bauer and Catherine Masciola. — 1st ed.
p. cm.
Summary: Twelve-year-old Sawyer Brown, his sister Elvira, and friends head into the Mississippi bayou seeking "Ol' One Eye," the biggest, oldest, and meanest catfish around, in hopes of finding Sawyer's widowed mother's wedding ring, which was swallowed by a smaller fish.
ISBN 978-0-7614-6223-1 (hardcover) — ISBN 978-0-7614-6224-8 (ebook)
[1. Adventure and adventurers—Fiction. 2. Catfishes—Fiction. 3. Bayous—Fiction. 4. Family life—Mississippi—Fiction. 5. Mississippi—Fiction.] I. Masciola, Catherine. II. Title. III. Title: Fishtale.
PZ7.B3259Fis 2012
[Fic]—dc23
2011040131

Book design by Alex Ferrari
Editor: Robin Benjamin

Printed in the United States of America (R)
First edition
10 9 8 7 6 5 4 3 2 1

To Morgan, Jane, and Carmen

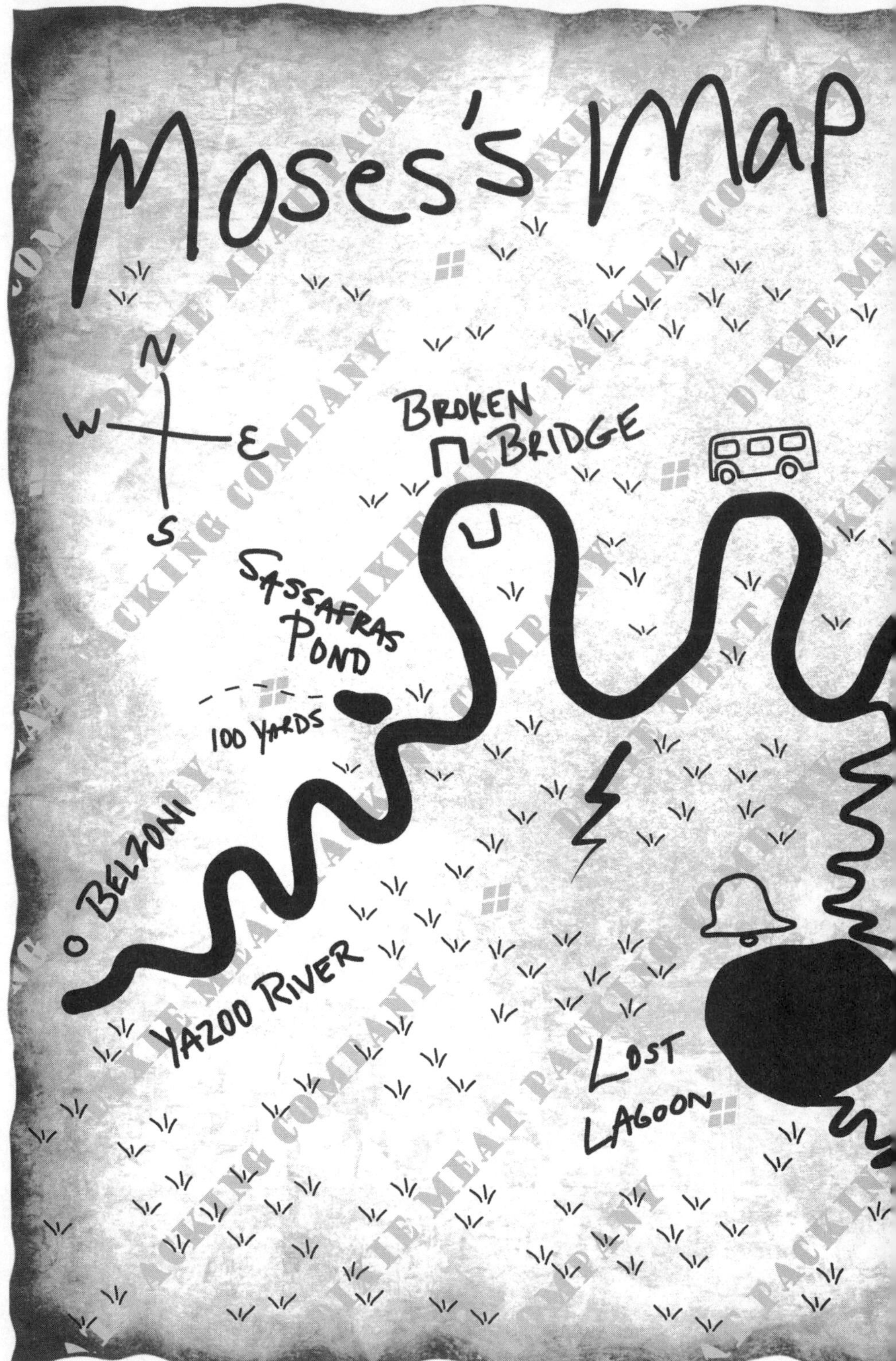
Moses's Map
N
W
E
S
BROKEN BRIDGE
SASSAFRAS POND
100 YARDS
BELZONI
YAZOO RIVER
LOST LAGOON

CONTENTS

1. FESTIVAL OF THE FISH — 1

2. CAT BITE — 9

3. DIXIE PRIDE — 18

4. ROSE — 24

5. CATFISH TIME — 30

6. FISHIN' EXPEDITION — 39

7. SASSAFRAS LANE — 48

8. UP THE YAZOO — 56

9. OL' TWO EYE — 67

10. DREAMLAND — 77

11. RED SKY IN MORNING — 84

12. SAILORS TAKE WARNING — 88

13. THE LAIR — 92

14. HOOKED — 104

15. GATOR BAIT — 115

16. MULBERRY SNOW — 123

17. LOST LAGOON — 131

18. DELTA BELLE — 140

19. EGG EYE — 151

20. CAT BAIT — 158

21. CAT FIGHT — 164

22. FOREVER IN BLOOM — 171

23. DOWN THE YAZOO — 179

24. MAIN STREET PIER — 190

25. FISHTALE — 194

1

FESTIVAL OF THE FISH

EVERYONE IN BELZONI, MISSISSIPPI, POPULATION 2,663, knew the story because Elvira Brown had told it about a trillion times. It had also been heard in other parts, meaning nearly every county in Mississippi, a half-dozen parishes in neighboring Louisiana, several counties in Alabama, Arkansas, and Missouri, and even a handful in Kentucky and Tennessee.

She'd told it over coffee and biscuits at the Humphreys Café. She'd told it before and after Thursday night choir practice at the First Baptist Church. She'd told it at the Bogg Street Y during Friday night bingo. She'd told it between Little League innings in the rough bleachers overlooking the town baseball diamond. And each and every time, she swore it was a tale told true.

What she couldn't swear to was how many of those listeners were believers.

And on this perfect April morning, sitting in her cramped and cluttered office at the World Catfish Museum on Magnolia Street, Elvira Brown was shortly going to tell it again.

Now, it wasn't like anyone was putting a bow and arrow to her head. She liked telling it. It *was*, after all, one heck of a fish tale.

A big-city-looking fellow drove his spiffy sedan through the broad and shady streets. Belzoni was a sleepy, old-timey kind of town on the banks of the Yazoo River. Newly planted gardens basked in sunlit patches between towering pecan and magnolia trees. It was the kind of town where kids still built tree house forts and underground bunkers to defend against their marauding crosstown rivals.

Most days, Belzoni's languid pace matched its peaceful setting. But this afternoon, Jackson Street was packed with folks parking their cars and streaming toward the town square. Stretched across the street was a wide banner:

18th Annual
WORLD CATFISH FESTIVAL

Big City found the only remaining space in the First Baptist Church parking lot. Soon, the lanky, bespectacled man was strolling among the booths and tables of a small town festival. The air was thick with the twang of amplified country blues guitar and the enticing aroma of what seemed to be a hundred recipes for catfish: grilled catfish, barbecued catfish, fried catfish, catfish gumbo, catfish nuggets, and catfish pie.

Downtown, the thick columns of the aging yellow brick courthouse were bedecked with vertical banners depicting scenes of catfish life. On the courthouse lawn, the musician had finished his set, and now an ensemble of locals in antebellum hoop skirts and frock coats hit the stage as a three-piece band—banjo, fiddle, and washboard—struck up a rural rendition of the Virginia reel.

Had Big City stayed to watch, he would have witnessed the coronation of a catfish queen, a catfish-eating contest, and a balloon-blowing goat which had nothing whatsoever to do with catfish but once again proved to be a popular favorite.

Instead, he wandered past the courthouse and on toward the World Catfish Museum. On the front lawn sprawled a scrap-metal sculpture of an enormous catfish. He shook his head. Now *that* was some fish. He snapped a few photos before heading inside. He was about to pull the door shut behind him when a big, shaggy, auburn-coated dog slipped through.

Inside, the museum was cool and dim, and Big City's eyes took a moment to adjust. He wandered among the catfish exhibits and paused before a display of mounted catfish of a dozen varieties.

"You know that cat?" asked a woman's voice.

He turned and found himself facing an outdoorsy-looking woman in her early thirties. Though she wore little makeup and had piled her hair up haphazardly in a bun, he saw that she was quite pretty, if she chose to make you think so. She pointed to a foot-long mottled brown fish.

"No earthly clue," he said.

"That's a brown bullhead. Your common cat." She pointed to another that Big City guessed was easily half the length of his car. It was deep blue.

He shook his head. "Moby Dick I know," he said, "but that one, afraid not."

"Moby Dick's a mammal," she replied. "That's a blue cat. World record's a hundred and forty pounds." Next she pointed to a bright yellow catfish.

"Let's see now, it's yellow, so there's a clue. I'm guessing—yellow cat?"

"Also called a shovelhead or flathead. Guess there's not much catfishing in the Big Apple, is there?" she said.

"About as much as there are bagels in the bayou. But I like fish."

"Me, too. It runs in the family."

"Bernie Singer, *New York Times*," he said, extending his hand. "The paper sent me down to do a story . . ."

They shook hands. "Elvira Brown," she said. "Got a call you'd be coming in this morning. I run our little museum here. Nice to meet'cha, Yankee."

Elvira led the way through a door marked Staff Only. The auburn dog came out of nowhere and squeezed through her legs. Bernie followed them down a corridor to another door with a nameplate which read *Elvira Brown, Curator.* She stepped aside and ushered the reporter into her office.

Bernie stopped to soak up his surroundings. A massive rolltop desk dominated the room. The heavy oak was buried under books and magazines and paperwork, drawers open, nooks and crannies overflowing.

Against the far wall, a rough cedar table displayed an enormous animal skull. Its massive jaws were agape.

"Make yourself at home," Elvira said. Bernie looked around, but there was no place to sit.

"Whoops," she said.

She stepped to a cane rocking chair and hefted the hollow shell of a snapping turtle, every bit as large as a trash can lid, and placed it on the floor beside a set of doggie bowls. Bernie returned to eyeballing the skull.

"I'm guessing you already know what that is," Elvira teased.

"If I guessed some kind of dinosaur, would I even be close?" Bernie asked.

"Close enough," Elvira replied. She bent toward a small fridge under a water cooler and removed a pair of ice-cold Yoo-hoos. "It's a gator."

Bernie was still soaking up the room when she handed him a Yoo-hoo. "Cool you off," she said.

Elvira lowered herself into the chair behind her desk. She let him get his fill of the room.

To the right stood a tall bookcase. The top shelf held a

folk art sculpture of dancing beavers behind a row of clay cookie jars.

To the left stood a row of glass-fronted cabinets filled with fossils, curios, bones, and other specimens. Hanging on the wall behind her desk were two diplomas: a Bachelor of Science in Wildlife Biology from Mississippi State and a Master of Natural History from Tulane.

A decorative antique scale balanced atop a stack of dusty leather volumes on Elvira's desk. Someone's home-made banjo leaned in a corner. Vintage blues records were scattered beside an old record player.

Bernie's eyes continued to roam. He saw a white-throated snake in a jar of formaldehyde. A stuffed, mangy lynx crouched on a log. A diorama of two large bass stalking a smaller prey fish was contained in a glass-sided coffee table before a ratty couch.

"My brother, Sawyer, gave me that for a graduation present."

"The couch or the coffee table?" Bernie asked.

Elvira beamed a cute smile.

"Unusual, to say the least," Bernie said, then added, "Quite a collection you've got. Reminds me of the Museum of Natural History. Growing up in Manhattan, my parents used to drop me off there about every other Saturday."

They unscrewed the caps on their Yoo-hoos. Wisps of compressed air erupted from the bottles like cold smoke. They sipped.

A frayed wicker ceiling fan, its blades shaped like palm

fronds, whirred overhead. The breeze lifted their hair. Papers rustled.

"So, Mr. Singer—" Elvira started.

"Bernie."

"So, Bernie—"

Bernie took another sip of his Yoo-hoo, then leaned forward. "You wouldn't happen to have a good fish story, would you?" he asked. "Something original. I've already heard about the one that got away." He chuckled.

The dog waited expectantly until Elvira poured a splash of Yoo-hoo into a water bowl. "This here's General Leigh. She has expensive taste." General Leigh eagerly helped herself to the flavored water.

Elvira settled back in her chair. Her blue eyes sparkled. "You sure you have time for this? Might take a while."

"That's what they pay me for," said Bernie. He opened his jacket and removed a tape recorder. Elvira cleared a space on her desk. Bernie switched it on. "Whenever you're ready," he said.

Elvira took her time sipping her drink and gathering her thoughts. General Leigh slumped on the cool linoleum. Bernie followed Elvira's gaze to another glass display case where odds and ends were arranged on shelves lined with faded red velvet. A warped harmonica. Wire rim spectacles. A rusty dog tag shaped like a bone. A silver thimble, a broken compass. A Confederate belt buckle, a tarnished bracelet. An ancient padlock. Assorted bottle caps, and old coins. A timeworn Barbie doll sat on a Barbie lunch box. A squashed accordion leaned against the display case. Propped atop the case was a cardboard box illustrated with a Mississippi paddlewheeler.

Finally she began: "Back when I was a kid, right around here, my momma ran a catfish farm . . ."

2

CAT BITE

Elvira Brown was standing on a chair, leaning over a goldfish bowl on her dresser. A pink wad of bubble gum, stuck to a safety pin, attached to a string, tied to a pencil, hovered over the bowl. She usually fed her pet a nutritious, balanced diet of fish flakes. But today, Elvira was teaching her Barbie how to fish. "Here, fishy, fishy, fishy," she whispered.

Across the hall, her big brother, Sawyer, was using a magnifying glass to inspect a paddlewheel he had just finished constructing for his latest model boat, the Mississippi sternwheeler *Robert E. Lee*, circa 1870.

Any minute now, their mother would be calling them to breakfast, and then to chores. There was no school today—summer vacation would last another precious month—but chores came before play on a farm.

Sawyer and Elvira both had responsibilities, and each was given a modest salary, most of which went into their college funds. Being the oldest, Sawyer was expected to run the family farm one day, just as his parents and grand-parents, and even his great-grandparents, had done.

Other than his family duties, Sawyer wasn't much different than any other twelve-year-old rural Mississippi boy. He was perhaps a little too skinny, though he had plenty of appetite. His mom said he was "growin' like a weed." He had brown hair like his dad and freckles like his mom. He enjoyed riding bikes, playing baseball, and building model boats, but most of all, Sawyer Brown loved to fish.

Elvira loved her dolls, especially her Barbie, but she also loved hanging out with Sawyer and his friends. And a nine-year-old Delta girl had to be pretty tough to hang out with twelve-year-old boys, even if one of them was her brother.

She wasn't half bad at baseball, and maybe that's why the boys—though they ditched her once in a while—would more often let her tag along to play outfield, or to go fishing. Like her brother, Elvira Brown loved to fish.

Downstairs in the kitchen, Rose Brown was making breakfast. She hummed while she worked, her bare feet hurrying across the pine plank floor. She glanced at the rooster-shaped clock above the stove.

"Sawyer! Elvira! Breakfast!" she called.

Like her children, Mrs. Brown had grown up eating breakfast in this big farmhouse kitchen. The house had been in her family for four generations. A large round oak table sat near the open window. The oak chairs had been made by her grandfather decades ago. Chintz curtains rustled in the breeze. In a corner was the original woodstove, sitting cold at this time of year. On a sideboard, a carved soapstone water buffalo teapot was planted with flowers.

Mrs. Brown laid out a trio of burger buns on the counter and returned to the skillet she was tending.

"Sawyer! Elvira! Let's move it!" she called.

The rusty pickup rattled along a dirt levee which ran between the rectangular ponds of the Browns' catfish farm. Mrs. Brown was behind the wheel, munching a catfish burger.

"C'mon, you two. Eat," she instructed. "Stop looking like I just ate the family cat."

Sawyer and Elvira eyed the catfish burgers that their mother had tossed on the dashboard. "We don't have a cat," said Elvira. "Just catfish. Millions."

"Jillions," said Sawyer.

Mrs. Brown gestured at their sandwiches. "Zillions— minus these three. Now eat, 'fore they get cold."

"I'm sick of catfish," complained Sawyer. "Catfish for breakfast. Catfish for lunch. Catfish for supper."

"Catfish for Christmas," Elvira chimed in. "Catfish for Thanksgiving. Catfish for birthdays."

"Mmmm, birthdays," Mrs. Brown said, teasing. "Now that's something I hadn't thought of. Catfish cake. Yum."

"Yeah, with catfish ice cream," said Sawyer, getting into the spirit. "Finger-lickin' good."

"And catfish candy!" piped up Elvira. "So good it makes you wanna lay down and *screeaam!*"

Sawyer unscrewed the top of a thermos and took a swig of lemon-lime Kool-Aid. Just then, the pickup hit a rut, and Sawyer was doused down the front of his shirt.

"Rats!" he exclaimed.

Elvira giggled.

The pickup stopped beside one of the catfish ponds. In the distance, a low green horizon signaled the beginning of the bayou. Catfish ponds were far from ordinary, but a brood pond, which this one happened to be, was altogether another kettle of fish.

The first thing you'd notice about a brood pond would be the gently bobbing corks that littered the surface. What you couldn't see were the hundreds of ten-gallon milk cans tethered just below. Male cats favored these dark holes, just the sort of places a papa cat would seek in the wild. He'd pick a cozy nook that would attract a mama cat to lay her eggs. Thousands of sticky eggs. Then the mama cat would swim away, leaving the papa behind to guard the nursery.

A scarecrow guarded one side of the pond. An over-turned tin pail served as its head, with painted black eyes, a red nose, and a toothy mouth. A ratty straw hat was nailed to its head. And nesting atop the hat was a sullen cormo-rant. Cormorants—big, nasty, fish-eating birds common in those parts—were always scouting for a meal.

It was impossible to tell the birds apart, but to Sawyer, the one roosting atop the scarecrow was always the same, the ringleader, overseeing a hungry flock lurking all around the levee, warming their wide gray wings in the sun.

Sawyer and Elvira tried to chase the birds off as Mrs. Brown pulled on a pair of fireman-yellow rubber gloves. They soon gave up the chase and removed a patched inner tube from the pickup bed. After loading it with an ice chest, they launched their egg collector into the pond.

"Mom, can I help run the cans?" pleaded Elvira.

"I'd say that's up to Sawyer, sweetheart. He's responsible for the duty roster."

"Sawyer? Can I, can I, can I, please?"

Sawyer looked at his mother. Their eyes met.

Elvira noticed his hesitation. She knew that the duty roster used to be part of their father's job. Sometimes Sawyer seemed uncomfortable when their mom reminded him, but he never hesitated to pull rank on Elvira when he felt like it.

Mrs. Brown gave Sawyer an encouraging nod.

Sawyer turned to his sister. "Alright," he said, "but be careful sticking your hand in with those males."

"I ain't scared of no stupid fish. Ain't scared of no males, neither," Elvira declared.

Sawyer found two pairs of extra gloves in the pickup. The pair he slipped into once belonged to his father. They were too big for his young hands but were nothing compared to the gloves Elvira wore. Her oversized mitts looked better suited to the Creature from the Black Lagoon than to a girl soon to enter the fourth grade.

Mrs. Brown scooted down the levee and waded into the pond. She tied the inner tube to her waist with a rope. Sawyer and Elvira joined her. The Brown family began "running the cans"—collecting the fish eggs from the submerged milk cans.

Elvira knew what Sawyer meant about being careful. Male catfish were aggressive about protecting their nests. Lots of Delta folk had been bitten or finned by ornery cats. She entered the warm shallow water and waded to one of the floating corks and hauled up a rope. She struggled to keep her balance as she tried to bring up a can that was almost half her size and weight. After tipping out the water, she eased her other hand into the saucer-sized hole at the top.

"I don't feel anything," she said.

Sawyer hauled up his own can and poured out the bluish green water. A plump papa cat spilled out. He stuck his hand in the can and felt around.

"Try this one," he instructed his sister.

Elvira sloshed over, dipped her hand in the can, felt around, and brought out a rubbery lemon-colored egg mass. She held it up proudly, displaying her find.

"Eggs!" she shouted. She waded to the egg collector and deposited the eggs.

"You're learnin', Vi," her brother said approvingly.

Mrs. Brown hauled up a can, poured out the water, stuck her hand in, and felt around.

"Yeooowww!!!" she hollered, jerking back. A two-pound catfish was still clamped to her gloved fingers. She waded to the levee and tugged at the cat with her free hand. But the fish wouldn't let go. "Sawyer—" she called.

Sawyer and Elvira quickly waded over and climbed out. Sawyer took hold of the slippery cat and tugged, but the fish still wouldn't let go. He tried again, this time giving the fish a light conk on the head. The cat finally released its grip and dropped to the ground. The glove came free and fell to the dirt. One of its fingers was missing.

"OH, NO—!"

"Mom, you okay?" Sawyer asked.

Sawyer and Elvira looked at their mother's hand where the catfish had latched on. A row of tiny teeth marks encircled her ring finger. Pinpricks of blood had begun to ooze.

"My wedding ring!" she cried frantically. "It's gone!"

Sawyer pointed to the flopping fish. "Catch him! Quick!"

Sawyer and Elvira stumbled over each other, groping for the cat, but it flipped out of their grasp and lay twitching at the edge of the pond. Just one more flop and it would be right back in the pond, most likely never to be seen again until it appeared on someone's supper plate.

Sawyer waved Elvira back and began to steal up on the catfish. He held his breath. The cat was now within arm's reach. He lunged. But he was a heartbeat too late. A waiting cormorant had seen its chance. The bird flapped across the pond, swooped low, scooped up the cat, and flew off.

The Brown family could only watch as the bird sailed out over the pond and off to the horizon until it shrank to a tiny smudge of black. Then it was gone.

The cormorant skimmed the treetops of the dense wetland and came to rest on a lofty bough of a cypress overlooking the twisting course of the Yazoo River. Once perched, it wasted no time swallowing the fat cat in a single gulp.

The greedy bird, still hungry for dessert, took wing again, following the winding watercourse. Finding just the right spot, it settled on a patch of sunlit water. Its practiced eyes immediately spied movement beneath the surface, a school of blue gill passing through a grid of shafting sunlight. The bird made a short jump before it dove, a perfectly streamlined entry into the water.

The school scattered, no longer all for one and one for all, but every fish for itself. The cormorant changed course, pursuing a solitary target, like a lioness cutting a zebra from the herd. The desperate fish darted right and left. The streaking bird matched it zig for zag.

The fish angled for the sheltering mouth of a decaying cypress trunk that lay half buried on the muddy bottom. The bird banked and followed. The fish disappeared into the black trunk. The raptor was close behind when an impossibly wide, whiskered mouth in a broad, pale face burst from the log tunnel, scarfed down fish and bird, and then sunk back into the dark of the log.

Back at the pond, Mrs. Brown sat on the open pickup gate while Sawyer wrapped a Band-Aid around her bleeding ring finger.

"Does it hurt?" asked Elvira, wincing.

"I'm okay, hon," Mrs. Brown said sadly as they drove away.

But she wasn't. She wasn't okay at all.

3

DIXIE PRIDE

Sawyer and Elvira bounced up and down in the pickup as their mother drove along the dusty road toward the Dixie Pride Catfish Plant. They passed through the main gate and steered toward a corrugated aluminum building with a sign that proclaimed "Dixie Pride Tasting Shed."

"Whew," said Mrs. Brown, wiping her arm across her forehead. "It's as hot as a billy goat in a pepper patch!"

Inside the shed, Moses Adams was preparing a tasting lesson. His sixty-eight years on the Mississippi Delta had been hard ones, and those years were etched deeply in the creases of his dark face. His wiry hair was more gray than not, and he liked to say that it appeared he'd end up having about as many teeth as he'd started with. But his black eyes still twinkled, especially when he was instructing his young grandson in the fine art of cat tasting, or more precisely, cat smelling.

Today Moses was feeling his age more than usual, but he paid no mind to his creaky joints, being thoroughly caught up in the lesson. His grandson, Waldo Adams, had the dark skin and wiry hair of his grandfather, but had acquired his nickname from his own special trait. Waldo—commonly known as Nose due to the significant size of his sniffer— was seated at a table, blindfolded. Grandpa Moses never gave a tasting lesson without the blindfold.

"Now let's say this cat farmer brings his fish in," began Moses. "Wants you to do a taste test. But you been tastin' fish all day. Hundreds of 'em. Just one more taste of pond cat and you'll explode. So whatchoo gonna do?"

"Start using my sniffer?" guessed Nose, who, of course, already knew the correct answer a hundred times over, but enthusiastically played along.

"Kee-rect!" said Grandpa Moses gleefully. "Now, first, the easy part."

Moses picked up a pair of meat-cutting scissors and a small catfish. Snip!—he chopped the fish in half, letting the head drop into a barrel. The other half he placed in one of three brown paper sacks on his desk. He turned to a cabinet where he kept all manner of odiferous objects. Casting an eye over his shoulder to check on Nose's blindfold, the old man ran his gnarled fingers through the jumble in the cabinet.

"Yeauupp," he muttered to himself as he selected an old

leather shoe for the second sack, and a dried-out rat carcass for the third.

"Now comes the true test," he announced, as he popped all three sacks into a toaster oven and set the timer.

Rose Brown parked the pickup outside the tasting shed. A rangy mutt came trundling up to greet them. "It's Rusty," exclaimed Elvira, spotting Nose's dog as she jumped out of the truck. "Here, Rusty! Come on, boy!"

Sawyer opened the tailgate for his mom, who took hold of the ice chest and began dragging it out of the truck. Suddenly, Mrs. Brown gasped and dropped the chest. Out spilled ice, three Yoo-hoos, and a solitary catfish.

"Mom—?" said Sawyer, ignoring the spill and putting his arm around her. "You okay?"

"It just slipped—"

Rusty bounded up and began sniffing the fish. "No, Rusty! Scat!" scolded Mrs. Brown, as the dog licked the slippery fish and tried to pick it up in his mouth.

Elvira took hold of Rusty's collar. "Come on, Rusty," she said, pulling him off.

Sawyer scooped the ice and Yoo-hoos back into the cooler and tossed the fish on top. "I can carry it, Mom," he said, closing the lid. Mrs. Brown smiled wearily.

Bing! The toaster oven was done. Moses pulled out a sack, opened it, and placed it in front of his blindfolded grandson. "Now let's see if you got the gift," he said.

Nose leaned forward and took a powerful sniff. "Hmmm. Kinda funky. Dead giveaway." He sniffed again. "I'm smelling algae. This fish musta turned green."

Moses shook his head and tossed the shoe into the barrel.

Nose grinned. The thud of the rejected "fish" boosted his confidence. "Next!" he cried.

Moses slid the next sack in front of Nose, who leaned in close and took a long, deep sniff of dead rat. "Mmmm," Nose said. "Now this is one fine fish." He sniffed again. "Mmmmmmm. I'd say this cat's right on-flavor. Pretty good eatin'."

Moses sighed. "Nose, you're battin' a thousand."

At that moment, the door opened and in trooped the Brown family with Rusty and the cooler.

"Well, look who's here!" Moses smiled.

"Hiya, Nose," said Sawyer.

"Hey, Saw," said the blindfolded Nose.

He and Sawyer were soon to begin the seventh grade at Humphreys County Junior High. Their friendship had begun several years before at the annual Catfish Races of the Mississippi State Fair.

Each contestant had been sponsored by an organization from the surrounding towns. Sawyer had found a sponsor in his Boy Scout troop. Nose had been sponsored by a Belzoni barbershop.

Sawyer had graciously allowed Elvira to name his would-be contender. She opted for Samson. Entirely by chance, Nose had named his catfish Goliath. Sawyer had fished his cat from one of the Brown family ponds. Nose had fished his straight from the Yazoo. Nose was wearing a T-shirt from Sawyer's favorite bush league baseball team, which had topped the AA league in the previous season. They talked baseball while waiting for the race to begin.

Neither boy's cat finished in the top three. For that matter, neither fish bothered to participate in a sporting fashion. Samson leapt and splashed into an adjoining lane and swam in the opposite direction. Goliath refused to participate entirely, lollygagging behind the starting line while fanning the water with his fins. Both fish proved a disappointment, but a friendship was born.

Nose removed his blindfold and peered into the sack. "A dead rat?" he muttered. "Dangit!" He hadn't won the sniffing game since getting hit in the snout by a ball during Little League tryouts that spring.

"Hi, Grandpa Moses, Nose," said Mrs. Brown. Everyone called Moses "Grandpa."

"How are you today, ma'am?" said Moses.

Mrs. Brown slumped into a chair and wiped her brow again. "Been a long day. You got time to check this sample?"

Moses removed the catfish from the chest and slapped it on the cutting table. But before he even took a slice— "Phewee," he said, shaking his head. "This cat's got dog breath. Where's this fish been?" Everyone turned to Rusty, who whimpered and slunk out of the shed. "Should've known," said Moses. "You got another sample, ma'am?"

Mrs. Brown sighed weakly and shook her head. "We've gotta go back and get another one then?"

"I'm real sorry, Mrs. Brown. I'm sure your pond's fine. But I gotta follow the rules before I can okay a buy."

Mrs. Brown stood up slowly. "It's alright," she said. "Come on, kids. Let's see if we can get this done before dark."

Sawyer carried the cooler back out to the truck, and the Brown family piled into the cab. Moses and Nose waved to them from the doorway as the truck started toward the main gate.

"Durn that ol' dog!" said Mrs. Brown.

"But he's so cute, Mom," said Elvira.

"He is at that—" began her mother, and then she cried out, grasping her side in pain. "Ahhh—"

The truck veered back toward the shed as Mrs. Brown slumped to her side. Sawyer clutched the wheel and struggled to control the steering, but he couldn't get his leg over the gearshift to slam on the brake, and the truck was heading straight for the shed, where Moses and Nose had gone back inside. Sawyer grabbed the parking brake and pulled hard, stopping the truck with a lurch just as Mrs. Brown regained her senses.

"Quick thinking, Saw," Mrs. Brown said softly, laying a trembling hand on her son's shoulder. They'd barely missed plowing right into the shed.

4

ROSE

Sawyer, Moses, and Nose sat in the hallway of the plant infirmary. Through an open door, they could see Mrs. Brown lying in a bed. The nurse was with her. Elvira had grown restless and wandered off.

The nurse came out of the sickroom. "She's resting now. I've called for Doc Marsh. You can go in."

Sawyer went to fetch his sister. She stood at the end of the hall, in front of a picture window overlooking the main processing room. A long conveyor belt moved an endless flow of catfish across the plant floor.

"It's 'cause of that dang fish, Vi," he said. "The one that bit her and took her ring." He stared glumly down at his feet. "I just know it is," he muttered. "C'mon," he said, taking his sister's hand.

As they walked back toward their mother's room, they passed the nurse, who sat at a desk making notes in a file. Sawyer stopped.

"I know what's wrong with her," he said.

"Oh? You do?" inquired the nurse gravely.

"She got bit by a catfish. I think maybe she got rabies or something."

"Fish don't carry rabies, son," said the nurse kindly. "Cats carry rabies. Not catfish." Sawyer considered this piece of information. He just knew his mom's sickness had something to do with that fish bite.

"You sure?" he asked.

"It's probably just a fainting spell. Temperature out there's toppin' a hundred today. Doc Marsh'll fix her up right quick," the nurse said. "Why don't y'all have Moses take you home? Go on now. Don't you worry."

Moses and Nose waited in the hall while Sawyer and Elvira returned to their mother's room. She seemed to be asleep. "Shhh," whispered Sawyer, putting his finger to his lips. He stood at the bedside, lost in thought.

A sunbeam shafted through the window blinds, casting a small pool of light on the cracked linoleum floor. Overhead, a tubular ring of fluorescent light buzzed softly. Above the sickbed hung a painting of an angel with a shining halo. Sawyer looked down at his mother's hand, at the Band-Aid wrapped around her finger where her wedding ring used to be.

• • •

Sawyer thought back to a day three and a half years before: the day his father had gone away. The family had gotten up at the crack of dawn because Mr. Brown had to take an early bus. Mom cooked a special breakfast casserole, Dad's favorite, and they all sat down together to eat.

Afterward, Sawyer followed his dad as he took the green canvas duffle bag out to the porch. Then Mr. Brown bent close so he could talk to Sawyer eye-to-eye, man-to-man. He put his hands on Sawyer's shoulders. "You help your momma, son," he said. "And look after your sister."

"Yes, sir," Sawyer had said solemnly.

"Sawyer," he'd said, looking deep into his son's eyes, "I love you."

"I love you, too, Dad," said Sawyer, throwing himself into his father's arms. His father held him for a long time. Sawyer didn't want to let go, partly because he didn't want his dad to go away, and partly because he didn't want him to see that his eyes were wet. But when they finally pulled apart, Sawyer saw that his dad's eyes were wet, too.

Sawyer never forgot that moment, never forgot what he saw in his father's face that day—how hard it was for him to leave them, how much he loved and would miss them. Sawyer also saw that his dad was afraid. Afraid of not getting to come back home.

• • •

The following year, on a cold, windy February day, two men came to the farm. They wore fancy uniforms under their billowing overcoats and looked very uncomfortable. When Mrs. Brown saw them coming up the porch steps, she sent Sawyer to take Elvira upstairs. He did as he was told, but he knew why the men had come.

After a while, the men drove away and Rose Brown came upstairs. Her eyes were red and her face was white. She pulled both the children onto her lap and told them that their father had gone to heaven.

Now, in Mrs. Brown's sickroom, Sawyer stared at the Band-Aid around his mother's ring finger and he knew he *had* to do *something*.

"She was fine until that fish took her wedding ring," said Sawyer quietly.

Grandpa Moses poked his head in the door and said, "C'mon, kids, I'll take y'all home. Your momma's gonna be fine. Sun'll shine bright on her come mornin'."

But come morning, the sun didn't shine any brighter, no brighter at all—not that morning, or the ones that followed.

Sawyer sat slumped on the front lawn next to a washtub filled with water. His model paddlewheeler was bobbing on the surface, but he no longer felt any enthusiasm for the project. He glanced up at his mom, dozing on the porch swing. Despite the heat, she was swaddled in a blanket. She'd grown noticeably thinner in the two weeks since the fish bite. She had dark circles under her eyes, even though she spent much of her time resting.

Elvira brushed away a milkweed bug that had settled on her mother's hair. Mrs. Brown opened her droopy eyes. "Sawyer, come here."

Sawyer shuffled toward the porch.

"Starting this weekend, there's gonna be some changes 'round here," she said.

"What's happening this weekend?" he asked warily.

"Well, for starters, your aunt Sarah is coming down. She'll help out while I go into the hospital for a few more tests. And she's bringing your cousin—"

"Mom, *please*—"

"Truman? Oh, boy!" Elvira interrupted. "Truman's coming!" She jumped up and down.

The Browns had been to visit the Wilsons several times at their spacious home in Memphis, Tennessee, just across the Mississippi state line. Truman's father was a Professor of Pharmacology at the University of Tennessee, and his mother was a registered nurse. They had a swimming pool, but Sawyer much preferred the Yazoo.

Sawyer bolted up the porch steps. "Mom, we can handle things around here without them. You don't have to do anything. Vi and I can do it. I can drive the truck—keep the books—and we both know how to run the cans—right, Virus?" He glared at his sister.

"Yeah, we can do it," she said reluctantly.

"They'll both be here for the summer," said Mrs. Brown firmly. "And I'm counting on you two to be proper hosts. And Sawyer, please don't call your sister Virus."

"Yeah, don't call me Virus," said Elvira.

"Aw, Mom," complained Sawyer. "Don't I get a say?"

"Sawyer, please. I'm sure you'll survive."

She looked so frail and exhausted, Sawyer couldn't bring himself to argue more. He plopped down on the porch step, sighing miserably.

5

CATFISH TIME

GRANDPA MOSES'S OLD STATION WAGON WAS PARKED beside a catfish pond. He sat on the open gate between Sawyer and Nose, teaching them how to play slide guitar with a weathered bottleneck. Sawyer was in a funk. He was in no mood for learning. Nose took the guitar and began working the slide.

"I didn't know better, Nose, I'd swear you done sold your soul at the crossroads." Moses beamed, referring to a well-known Delta legend about a musician who made a pact with the Devil to become the greatest blues guitarist of them all.

Nose continued working the tune, "Catfish Blues."

"Hear that, Saw?" Nose said. "Grandpa thinks I'm a regular Robert Johnson."

But Sawyer's mind was elsewhere. He gazed out over

the ponds, watching a great blue heron skim the water's edge to snag a fat bullfrog. The bird headed for the bayou with its supper.

"Where do they go, Moses?" Sawyer asked. "What happens to 'em?"

"Same thing as'll happen to that frog. Somewhere out there, that bird'll end up a meal for somethin' else."

"Like a gator?" asked Nose.

"Could be," said Moses. "Them that lives off those waters, ends up in those waters."

"Ain't gonna happen to the Nose," proclaimed Nose, pointing to himself with his thumb. "Soon as I get my license, I'm burnin' rubber up Highway Forty-Nine."

"Oh, you might clear out," replied Moses with a knowing nod. "But you'll be takin' the Delta wit'ya."

They sat in silence for a while, listening to Nose tinkering with the guitar.

"Peace, fellas," said a voice coming toward them. It was a boy dressed in a riot of psychedelic color: tie-dyed T-shirt, bell-bottom jeans, bandana, and a peace-sign button.

"The circus must be in town. One of the clowns got loose," said Nose with raised eyebrows.

"Oh, man. It's my cousin," muttered Sawyer.

"Hey, Sawyer," said Truman. "Your mom said you'd be out here."

"Hi, Truman. Uh, this here's Nose and this—"

"Nose? I don't think I'm familiar with the nationality of your moniker."

Nose stared at Truman as if he'd just arrived from another planet.

"I think he's asking why they call you Nose," explained Sawyer.

"Take notes, Einstein," said Nose to Truman. "And keep your eyes on the sniffer." He leaned toward a nearby pond and sniffed deeply. "I smell catfish!" he announced.

Truman gestured at the ponds. "But, this is a catfish farm. There're catfish everywhere."

"Then I rest my case," said Nose.

Sawyer rolled his eyes. He didn't know which of them was crazier. "Uh, and this is Grandpa Moses. Moses, my cousin, Truman."

Moses extended a hand.

"Charmed to make your acquaintance, sir," said Truman, shaking his hand. "Well, what's on the menu for today? I'm starved for a little *joie de vivre.*"

Moses picked up the guitar. "Been teachin' the boys a little twelve-bar blues. You like music, Truman?"

"Music? You're talkin' to a guy who's memorized the chords to every twelve-bar blues song ever made. Heck, I live for music. Even brought my accordion. I'll go back and get it. We can jam."

"*Joie de vivre,*" said Moses, watching Truman run off. "Somethin' you could use a little of, Sawyer."

"Yeah? What is it?" Sawyer asked, not really caring.

"French, I think. Hear them Cajuns say it all the time. Kinda hard to define, though. But it's the best cure for what ails ya, that's for sure. I got some back at my place, if you're interested."

Sawyer mulled over the offer. "Think I'll pass."

"Yeah, you're probably right. A weekend hoedown with your cousin is more to your likin'. Anyways, I got work to do. You change your mind, I'll be home all evening."

Moses climbed into his car and drove off.

Late that evening, a swollen moon, just past full, was rising over the trees. Sawyer Brown walked along the levee running between the misty fish ponds. He was approaching a ramshackle sharecropper's cabin. Much of the cabin was covered in thick kudzu, also known as "the plant that ate the South." An aluminum boat lay among the tangled vines.

The overgrown yard was littered with scrap metal. Sawyer started when he spotted a shape amid a dense carpet of invading weeds. But it was only a junk metal sculpture of a titanic catfish, under construction. Still, it had him rattled.

He knocked on the screen door. "Grandpa Moses," he said uncertainly. Nothing. He knocked again, louder. The door creaked open under his knuckles. "Mose—?" He stepped inside.

Sawyer entered a dim room of flickering shadows, swaying curtains, and the shifting shapes of Moses's scrap metal animal sculptures. A primping raccoon. A stealthy panther. An oval-eyed owl. Sawyer moved toward the kitchen. A supper plate piled with fish bones sat by the sink. "Moses?" he said again.

His gaze was drawn to an enormous pickle jar on a table. Moonlight streamed through the backdoor screen, casting an eerie glow on the jar. He peered into it. A white orb floating in milky pink fluid stared back at him. As Sawyer looked, a terrifying face began to form within the milky fluid. Contorted. Monstrous. Sawyer yelped.

"Whaaa!" He jumped back clear across the room before he realized it was Moses's face on the other side of the jar.

The old man shuddered. "Don't blame ya fer jumpin'. Dang thing still spooks the bee-geezus out of me."

Moses quickly covered the jar and its mysterious contents with a sheet of butcher paper. But somehow, perhaps by a trick of the moonlight, that eerie orb was still visible through the wrapping.

"Wh-what is it?"

"You don't want to know," Moses said. "Best you keep away from that thing." He steered Sawyer toward the back porch, where an oil drum was brimming with bait. "Wanted to show you a new stink bait I been workin' on," he said, pointing to the screen door. "Guaranteed to catch the big 'uns."

But Sawyer wasn't listening. That glowing orb had him thoroughly entranced.

"Thought you boys might like to be the first to give it a try—" Moses continued. But he saw the spell the jar had cast. He smiled a crooked smile, reached over, and pulled off the butcher paper with a flourish. The two of them stood considering the peculiar object.

"It's a gator egg, right?" asked Sawyer.

Moses chuckled. "Ain't no egg. Look close. You'll never get no closer to Ol' One Eye than what's in that jar."

"Ol' One Eye?"

"You heard right. Ol' One Eye. The biggest, oldest, smartest, and *meanest* durn cat that ever swum the Yazoo. 'Course, before I got a piece of 'im, they called him by some other names. Nothin' I'd repeat in front of a boy."

"A piece of him?" asked Sawyer.

"Yep. That's his eye you're lookin' at."

Sawyer drew back, furrowing his brow.

"I got his eye," said the old man, "and he got my gold tooth." Moses pointed to a tooth-sized gap in his yellowed grin.

Sawyer tilted his head and stared at the jar. "Ain't no catfish eye that big. And if there is, how'd you get it?"

"That's the second thing you don't wanna know," said Moses.

"Ol' One Eye? Is he bigger than the hundred pounder that crazy poacher caught last year on the Yazoo?"

"Shoot, I reckon that eye alone weighs close to that."

Sawyer's breath whistled as they studied the eye from another angle. "Then Ol' One Eye must be huge . . ."

Sawyer turned to Moses. Their eyes met. Moses winked.

". . . very, very huge," they said in unison.

Sawyer's eyes widened at the thought of how big this cat must be.

"Trouble is, after this week, Ol' One Eye won't be nothin' but an old man's fish tale," said Moses.

"Why's that?"

Moses turned over the butcher paper. On the back was a faded hand-drawn map showing rivers, lakes, channels, bayous, and landmarks. "Army Corps of Engineers is building a dam," he explained. "Right here." Moses pointed a gnarled finger to a spot on the crinkled map. "And Ol' One Eye's nest is somewhere up here," he added, tapping another spot. "Come next week, this'll all be one big lake. Then he could be anywhere. And then—this map'll be useless."

Sawyer turned back to the glowing orb.

"You feel it, don't you?" asked Moses. "I know I still do. 'Course, the power's a lot stronger when you're young. And I ain't young no more. But you—"

"Power? What power?"

"The power of Catfish Time."

"Huh?"

"You never heard of Catfish Time?" asked Moses. Sawyer shrugged. "When you're on Catfish Time, miracles is possible, Sawyer. When you're on that river with jus' your pole, your buddies, and—"

"Miracles, huh?" Sawyer scoffed. "Like maybe Catfish Time can save my mom. Yeah, right."

"Maybe so, maybe not," said Moses.

Sawyer snorted.

"See. That's your problem, Sawyer. You don't believe no more. You don't feel the power."

"I feel something," said Sawyer. "Somethin' pullin' my leg."

"You gotta believe in Catfish Time if you want it to work. You gotta pick up that pole again. And get back on that river. You gotta row with the flow, son."

Sawyer made for the door. "Think I'll just row on outta here."

"Just as well. Ol' One Eye might be too much fish for a little kid."

Sawyer wheeled around. "I ain't no little kid!" he flashed. "I can do anything *you* can—and that includes catchin' the biggest, oldest, smartest, meanest durn cat that ever swum the Yazoo! And not just his eye, neither!"

"Sorry. Forgot who I was talkin' to," said Moses sincerely.

Sawyer yanked the map out of Moses's hand. "When do we go?" he demanded.

"We—? No, I'm past my time. But you—" Moses gazed through the screen door up at the moon. "—you and your buddies make a brave crew. You three could do it."

Sawyer looked out into the darkness. He thought of Truman twitching at every little night sound. He shook his head.

"No way. I pass." He started to leave.

"That's a shame. Was hopin' you boys would save me some of that treasure."

Sawyer stopped in his tracks. "Treasure?"

"That's right. If it glows, it goes—right into Ol' One

Eye's nest. This cat is one heck of a collector, Sawyer. And he's got good taste. I expect he's picked clean every sunken riverboat in these parts. You find Ol' One Eye, chances are you'll be a rich man." Moses stepped back and smiled. He watched as Sawyer turned to the glowing orb again.

After what seemed like a long time, Sawyer said, "Thanks, but no thanks, Moses," his voice barely audible as he handed the map back. "Think I'll stick with my first plan. I'll just row on outta here."

The boy turned and passed through the door into the Delta twilight.

6

FISHIN' EXPEDITION

THAT NIGHT, TRY AS HE MIGHT, SAWYER COULDN'T SLEEP. He lay in bed turning the idea of going after Ol' One Eye over and over in his mind. Sure, he'd told Moses he flat-out wasn't interested, but there was no question he was sorely tempted. Who wouldn't be? Under normal circumstances, he wouldn't have to think twice. But things weren't anywhere near normal. His mom was sick, and Sawyer had responsibilities. What would Dad have thought if Sawyer just up and left his family in search of a fish?

He sat up and fixed his gaze on the map taped to the wall above his dresser. Moonlight cast a glow on the various countries shaded in pastel hues. After his father left, Sawyer had frequented the Humphreys County Public Library on South Hayden Street, learning all about the part of the world where his father had gone to serve. The map was a foldout from the *National Geographic*.

Sawyer went to the dresser and removed a photo album from the top drawer. He climbed back in bed and by the light of the bedside lamp, he opened the album. On the first page was a dog-eared Polaroid of his dad, standing at the rail of a metal boat on a mud-colored river against a backdrop of towering palms. He wore a soldier's uniform and camouflage helmet. On the helmet was written a list of twelve months beginning with March. All were crossed out except the last. February. February was the month he was supposed to return to the Delta.

Beneath the helmet, Dad smiled back at him—and with good reason. He held aloft a whopper of a catfish, maybe a twenty, twenty-five pounder.

Sawyer studied the familiar image. The tired eyes, the exuberant smile. The free hand raised in a two-fingered peace sign. The soldier's belt and gear—knife, canteen, and other objects Sawyer couldn't identify.

Then something else caught Sawyer's eye, something he hadn't noticed before. He cocked his head and stared. He returned to the dresser to retrieve his magnifying glass and positioned the lens over the hand holding the fat catfish. There it was—a slim gold band matching his mom's wedding ring.

He carefully slid the picture from its plastic sleeve and turned it over. Printed in his father's hand were two words: *Catfish Time!*

Sawyer gasped. He sat turning the photo over and back, staring at the words, and staring at his father's image. At last, he returned the photo to its sleeve, switched off the light, and slipped beneath the covers. He was fighting tears and about to lose when he heard Aunt Sarah's voice drifting from down the hall.

"I'll raise them like they were my own."

Raise them? What were they talking about? Sawyer got up and padded silently to the door.

"Truman would love having a brother and sister," Aunt Sarah was saying.

"They love this farm—" he heard his mom say.

"We could turn it into a summer home. Maybe lease out the ponds—" Aunt Sarah replied.

And suddenly it was all too much. He was either going to cry or sink under a great wave of blackness. Sawyer grabbed a model ship from a shelf and sent it sailing across the room. It smashed into the wall and shattered into a thousand plastic shards. He tried to hold back his tears, but they came anyway. He rubbed his fists into his eyes and swallowed hard. "Not if I can help it," he vowed.

Sawyer pulled himself together and headed down the hall to his mother's room. Aunt Sarah was coming the opposite way with a concerned look. "What was that?" she asked.

"Nothing," said Sawyer. "Dropped my boat."

Aunt Sarah started to say something more, but

thought better of it when she saw his face. She watched him go to his mother's room, then sighed and went downstairs.

Sawyer approached his mother's bed. On her bedside table, among the pill bottles, was a display of framed photos. Sawyer and Elvira at various ages. Sawyer as a baby in his father's arms.

Rose Brown groped for the lamp with an unsteady hand and switched it on. In the last few days her illness had begun to sprint. Her skin was stretched like parchment, her eyes hollowed. She lifted her head from the pillows. Her voice was thick and slightly groggy.

"I hardly recognize you anymore, Sawyer. You're growin' faster than kudzu."

Sawyer took one of her skeletal hands in his. He looked at the band of pale flesh around her ring finger, and the fading bite marks.

"Mom, would you feel better if you still had Dad's ring?"

"Yes, sweetheart. I'd feel a lot better. But, like your daddy, they're both gone. Forever. You gotta learn to take the good with the bad. It's part of growin' up."

"Think you could get along without me for a few days?" Sawyer asked.

"Goin' fishin' with the boys, then?"

"No. I'm gonna save your life."

Mrs. Brown managed a weak smile. "Oh, is that all?"

"I'm gonna try."

"That's real sweet of you, Sawyer."

"Even if you say I can't, I'm gonna try anyhow. So you may as well give me permission."

"Then I guess I better give it. You and Nose have been out on your own before. But your cousin Truman—well, you two keep an eye on him. And I want you back here Sunday morning. Don't make me have to send someone looking for you."

"Yes, ma'am."

"Okay. Save my life, then," she said. "But get a good night's sleep first."

"Okay, Mom," he agreed. But he didn't leave.

"And take your slicker," she said. "Weatherman said it might rain."

"Okay," he said again. But still he didn't go.

"I love you, Mom," he said impulsively.

"I love you, too," she said. "Now get goin' 'fore I change my mind."

"I'm going," he said.

He backed away from the bed, turned, and was gone.

Sawyer snuck down the porch steps while the others slept. It was nearing midnight when he approached the sharecropper's shack for a second time that night. The porch light cast a yellow glow across that catfish sculpture. Before he could knock, the screen door creaked open.

"Can I see it again?" Sawyer asked before Moses—

who didn't seem at all surprised to see him—could speak. The old man held the door and Sawyer slipped past.

Sawyer stood before the glowing orb in the big jar.

"What about a ring, Grandpa Moses? A gold ring? You think Ol' One Eye'd go for a little bitty ring?"

"Gold, silver, you name it. You find Ol' One Eye, his stash'll be somewhere nearby," he replied.

Sawyer stared silently at the jar. "Are miracles really, really possible in Catfish Time, Moses?"

"Way I see it, if you can catch that one-eyed monster, there ain't nothin' in life that can lick ya."

"Then I guess I'll be needin' that map," Sawyer said, putting out his hand. But he hadn't needed to ask; Moses was already placing it in his open palm.

Sawyer folded and pocketed the map. "It ain't a question of *if*. It's just a question of *when*," he declared.

"Yeah-bob!" Moses exclaimed as Sawyer took off through the open door.

Moses followed the boy outside and watched him disappear into the night. The metal sculpture of the giant catfish glittered like gray bones in the moonlight. He went back inside, switched off the porch light, and shut the door.

He turned to the jar. Unscrewing the lid, he removed the white orb and, with a flick of his wrist, he cracked that pickled egg on the rim of the jar. And slowly, he began to peel off the shell. Finally, he took a bite.

"Maybe so," he said aloud as he chewed. "Then again, maybe not."

• • •

Dawn found Sawyer, Nose, and Truman seated around a kitchen table piled high with food, condiments, containers, and assorted odds and ends. Elvira, Mrs. Brown, and Aunt Sarah were still asleep. A transistor radio on the counter played country swamp music. They hummed along, hunched busily over their work.

Since visiting Moses the night before, Sawyer had given a lot of thought to what kind of bait would tempt that tremendous beast, how hard it would fight, what he would do with his share of the treasure, and whether it might actually include a golden ring.

Truman interrupted his thoughts. "So how big do you think he is?"

"Bigger than all of 'em," said Sawyer.

Nose snickered. "Grandpa's been telling that tale my whole life. My brothers and me quit buying it when we were little. That's why he's tryin' to sell it to you now, Saw."

"Then how come you're here making bait?" Sawyer countered.

"I figure I better keep an eye on y'all. Sort of a fishing guide, see?" said Nose.

"Yeah, right," said Sawyer. "I think you've got a nose for that treasure."

Nose shrugged.

"One thing I know for sure—a special fish calls for special bait," said Sawyer.

Each boy had his own idea of what might tempt a giant cat; each knew that worms, minnows, salami, and ordinary stink bait were out of the question.

Sawyer picked up a clothespin and, with a flourish, clamped it to his nose. He took a slice of Wonder bread out of a bag, unscrewed a jar of peanut butter, spooned out a gooey glob, and spread it on the bread. He laid on a dead frog and drowned it in ketchup. He sprinkled on some chewing tobacco, laid on another slice of bread, and rolled that foul sandwich into a mushy ball. Next he took a discarded bra he'd found in the trash, scissored off a cup, and inserted the mess. He folded the bra cup and stapled it shut. Then he inserted a big fishhook.

Meanwhile Truman, his nose plugged with cotton balls, was unfolding a sheet of butcher paper, revealing a slab of bloody liver. He weighed it on a kitchen scale and jotted down the information in a small notebook. He removed a dead mouse from a cigar box. Weighed it. Recorded the data in his notebook. He laid the mouse on top of the liver and sprinkled on some salt and pepper. He topped it off with some shaving cream, folded the mess, and sewed up the liver with needle and thread. Weighed it again. Recorded the data in his notebook. Then he inserted a big fishhook.

Nose hadn't bothered to stuff his broken sniffer. He spooned a can of dog food into the blender and poured in some Tabasco. He added spaghetti sauce, salad dressing, and a handful of dead flies scraped from a windowsill. A shot of Worcestershire sauce. A shot of motor oil. A green olive. He ran the blender for a few seconds, then poured the whole mess into a rubber chicken. He inserted his lucky rabbit's foot. Then he inserted a big fishhook.

Sawyer pushed back his chair and nodded at his team.

"Let's go fishing."

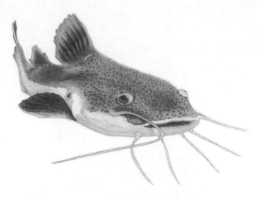

7

SASSAFRAS LANE

"—NINETY-FOUR–NINETY-FIVE–NINETY-SIX—" WITH MOSES'S
map in hand, Sawyer Brown led the way, counting off
carefully paced yard-long strides. The boys walked along
a country lane, towing Moses's aluminum rowboat on two
rusty wagons roped one behind the other. Piled in the boat
was a heap of fishing poles, tackle, camping gear, canteens,
and coolers, all crowned by Truman's accordion.

On either side of the lane, cotton crops stretched far and
wide. In the distance, willows marked the path of irrigation
ditches that flowed between the fertile fields.

Later, in the heat of the day, all the wildlife would be
napping. But now, in the cool of dawn, squirrels scampered
up tree trunks while birds scolded them crossly and flitted
among the treetops. Morning dew still clung to the weeds
and wildflowers.

Sawyer had already told Nose and Truman about the eye, and the map, and the possibility of a treasure, but he had withheld the true purpose of his quest. If and when the time was right, he would explain everything, but for now, it was enough to know they were seeking a monster cat.

"—Ninety-seven—ninety-eight—ninety-nine—" Sawyer counted.

The boys stopped. They had come to a storybook pond—not too big, not too small, just right for dipping a fishing pole. A deadfall of rotting logs crowded the far side.

Sawyer started dragging the rig to the pond. "C'mon," he said. "It's Catfish Time!"

"Ain't no way Ol' One Eye could be in there," said Nose. "Toilet bowl's got more water'n that."

Truman wrinkled his nose at the murky water. "Yechhh. And someone forgot to flush. Probably full of snakes, too."

"This is it!" Sawyer said. "It says so right on the map. One hundred yards down Sassafras Lane." He gestured dramatically. "See for yourself!" They passed the map from hand to hand, each inspecting Moses's notations.

"I tell ya, it ain't deep enough," said Nose, shaking his head.

"Only one way to find out how deep that pond is— and that's scientifically," said Truman as he whipped out a slide rule and began working it feverishly. Sawyer and Nose looked on, dumbfounded.

"You tellin' me that rubbin' them two sticks together's gonna tell us where Ol' One Eye is?" Nose said.

"Once I find the circumference of this pond, I'll convert the data with this slide rule. Then, to find how deep it is, it's just a matter of applying the—"

Sawyer had heard enough. While the others were arguing, he picked up a fist-sized rock and lobbed it way out over the pond.

KERSPLASH! Nose and Truman turned to the pond. Ripples were spreading out over the water.

"What was that?" said Nose.

"Didn't get a look at it," Sawyer responded. "But it must've been big. Real big."

For the moment, they were hooked, too.

A short time later, the boys were adrift in the middle of the pond, fishing lines in the water. Nose dug through the pockets of his overalls, produced a handful of balloons, and passed them around. Soon a brightly colored trio of balloon bobbers floated on the water.

Truman, his face covered with sunscreen, was unpacking goggles, fins, and a snorkel. Nose had changed into gaudy swim trunks, a loud Hawaiian shirt, straw hat, and cool shades. He lounged back with his feet up on the side of the boat, sipping a root beer. "This is the life!" he exclaimed.

Ordinarily, on such an expedition, the fishermen would sit back, soaking up the sun, imagining the life of a hand-to-mouth tumbleweed boy, living off the land, as free as the sky. But not today: today there was business at hand.

Sawyer pointed to the deadfall of floating logs and debris across the pond. "If Ol' One Eye's here," he said, "he's probably hidin' under them logs."

"Aye, aye, cap'n," said Nose as he rowed their craft closer and steadied it. They recast their lines.

Bored, Truman picked up his accordion and began to pump out a tune. "Since I saw her face—now I'm a believer—" he began.

"Hey, Einstein, you're scarin' the fish!" shushed Nose.

"Scarin' me, too." Sawyer laughed.

"You men have no sense of *joie de vivre*," said Truman. "That's your problem." He swung the accordion over his head and began playing it behind his back.

The boat rocked. Truman lost his balance, tripped over the seat board, and landed hard on his butt. Sawyer and Nose burst out laughing. Truman sat up, grinning sheepishly. Just then, they heard a muffled sound. The boys looked at each other. "What was that—?"

"Are we there yet?" asked a familiar voice.

They all jumped as the seat board popped open. Elvira emerged from a concealed hollow, wearing a bright yellow life jacket and clutching her Barbie lunch box. She yawned and looked around.

"Virus." Sawyer buried his head in his hands.

"Oh, man!" said Nose.

"Hey, *Waldo*," said Elvira. Nose blanched at the use of his given name.

"What? At least I'm not named after some disgusting germ," he retorted.

"No way you're coming, Virus," said Sawyer.

"Why not?" she whined.

"You're just a little girl."

"You're just a little boy."

"Mom will be worried sick."

"I left her a note."

"Virus—"

BANG! One of their balloons exploded. The boys quickly turned back to their lines. Sawyer's was sinking fast, and tightening. He gripped his pole and pulled hard. It wouldn't give an inch.

"We got him, Nose! We got him!" he shouted.

Nose grabbed ahold of the pole alongside Sawyer. Both fishermen strained.

"I smell him, Saw! I got Ol' One Eye's scent locked in! It's him, all right! The Nose knows!"

Truman grabbed ahold of the pole, too, and all three pulled as hard as they could. "I knew he was here!" said Truman. "I just forgot to factor the slope of the hypotenuse into the depth of the—"

SNAP! The line broke. The boys tumbled back, arms and legs entangled. As they stared out across the water, they saw it was only a small log that had snagged Sawyer's line. The log had torn free from the deadfall, dislodging other branches and debris.

All at once, the entire deadfall began to shift and

collapse. To their horror, they realized it was all being sucked down some kind of funnel. Everything was vanishing down a black hole! As the mass shifted, they could make out the yawning mouth of a huge drainage pipe, with water and detritus surging riotously in. It was as if someone had pulled the plug in a giant bathtub.

"Uh-oh," said Nose. "The Nose smells trouble."

"Ohhhh, rats!" said Sawyer.

"Row!" shrieked Elvira.

The boys were already grabbing their oars and paddling madly toward the shore. But the current was far too strong, and the boat was rapidly drawn closer and closer to the dark mouth of the pipe.

"Hang on," shouted Sawyer, tossing aside his oar and grabbing Elvira. "We're goin' in!"

They hollered wildly as the boat careened down the winding tunnel, scraping the corrugated metal sides as it hurtled along. They held on tight, their shouts and screams echoing off the tunnel walls. As they rounded a bend, Sawyer lost his grip on Elvira's hand, and she was bounced and tossed atop Truman's accordion, which wailed eerily through the dark passage.

Sawyer fumbled in his gear for a flashlight and switched it on. The jerking beam now illuminated their wild ride, revealing an obstacle course of Jurassic-sized, wall-to-wall spider webs as they plowed through.

It seemed forever that they were swept along with that

wave of surging pond water before a faint circle of light could be seen. It grew brighter until the castaways saw that they were about to be shot out of the rushing mouth of the pipe into who-knew-where.

"Eeeeaahhh!" they hollered as the boat was ejected through the spewing water and suddenly became airborne. The boat seemed to hang in midair before finally crashing down hard in the river below.

"Whooo-hooo!" shouted Sawyer. "What a ride! Everybody okay?"

Nose, Truman, and Elvira looked around and, realizing they were okay, began to laugh and whoop along with Sawyer.

"Check for spiders," cautioned Sawyer between laughs. They brushed the silky shrouds off each other's backs and inspected the boat and gear.

"Uhhh-ohhh," Nose said shakily, pointing to a banana spider sitting on his straw hat, which had fallen to the bottom of the boat. The poor spider, which must have been more scared and bewildered than they were, sat still as a stone, probably hoping not to be noticed. Elvira, who was closest, snatched up the hat and flung it over the side. "Hope it can swim," she said.

"Who cares!" said Truman.

"My hat!" said Nose.

They looked around and found themselves in the middle of a wide, muddy river. The pipe mouth, now well above them, projected from a steep embankment.

Nose gave a low whistle, realizing how far they'd fallen. "We must be somewhere up the Yazoo," said Truman. Sawyer consulted the map. "You can say that again." They took up their oars and began to row.

8

UP THE YAZOO

THE ADVENTURERS PADDLED UPRIVER, PUSHING DEEPER into the primordial swamp. A labyrinth of channels branched off in all directions. Thick curtains of Spanish moss hung heavy from bald cypress and weeping willow, cottonwood and maple. Exotic birdcalls came from high up in the trees. Giant dragonflies buzzed low over the slow-moving water. A hushed stillness enveloped the boat.

They rowed quietly past the sagging remains of a footbridge on either side of the river. Sawyer consulted the map.

"Broken bridge," he read aloud. It was one of the landmarks indicated on the map.

They looked at each other. Maybe old Moses's map actually *was* for real.

• • •

Upriver, the steaming silence of the swamp was as yet undisturbed by the approaching craft. A swamp rabbit nibbled furtively at tender shoots along the riverbank. A small green frog sprawled lazily atop a lily pad. The frog tensed as voices drifted in on the faint breeze. The rabbit bolted for his hole.

"I don't know," Truman was saying. "If Ol' One Eye is so big, then how come nobody's ever seen him?"

"Easy," said Sawyer. "'Cause he's way too big to be believed."

"Huh?" said Truman.

"No one comes out here lookin' for a fish that big. So if they do see him, they can't believe their eyes. And there's no camouflage better than that," said Sawyer.

"It's no wonder he got so big," said Elvira.

The boys continued rowing. Nose's oar splashed down almost on top of the lily pad, causing the little green frog to leap for his life. The boat glided on upriver.

After a time, they came upon an ancient cypress which long ago had been cleaved nearly in half by a lightning strike. Sawyer checked the map again.

"Look here," he said, pointing. A bolt of lightning was drawn on the map, just upriver from the broken bridge. Moses must have been referring to the lightning tree! They exchanged excited glances.

• • •

Farther upriver, a magnificent bobcat stood poised and motionless at the water's edge, ears perked and gaze focused intently on a nervous duck and her brood swimming hurriedly by. The approaching sound of hushed voices reached the bobcat's keen hearing.

"Yeah," Nose was saying. "People have a hard enough time believing in the hundred pounders that got away. Who's gonna believe they saw a fish ten times that big?"

"Nitwits? Like us?" joked Truman. They all joined in his laughter.

Realizing she'd never catch any lunch with such a racket disturbing her territory, the indignant bobcat padded off, heading deeper into the swamp.

"Think about it," Sawyer was saying. "If you saw a fish that big you'd keep it under your hat, too. Wouldn't want anyone thinking you're crazier than you are."

"Ol' One Eye couldn't have gotten that big without being smart," Elvira said. "He must be the smartest fish in the world,"

"We'll never catch him if he's that smart. Or that big," said Truman.

"Any catfish that big is too big *not* to fish for!" declared Sawyer.

The others nodded solemnly as the boat rounded a bend. The duck and her brood paddled behind a partially submerged rusted-out school bus and disappeared through an open window.

"Hey," said Sawyer, holding up the map and pointing again. "Look!"

Sure enough, a crude figure of a bus was drawn near a bend in the river. They all grinned. Moses's map must be right! They were definitely on Ol' One Eye's trail now!

By this time, it was well past noon, muggy hot and getting hotter. "Time for lunch," announced Sawyer. "Let's stop awhile under those trees."

They rowed toward the shady spot and tossed their mooring line over a branch. Bologna sandwiches, sodas, and chips were passed around.

Truman pointed to a ring-tailed creature on the opposite bank. "Look! A *Procyon lotor*. Or raccoon, to you gentlemen."

"That's no raccoon, Tru," Sawyer said. "That's a coatimundi. Check out the long snout."

"Yeah, shows you don't know everything," Nose said smugly.

"A *kwata-what*?" said Truman.

"Ko-WAH-ti-MUN-dee," Elvira pronounced carefully. "It's a snout-nosed mammal in the raccoon family. We learned about it in school."

"Cool," said Truman. Elvira beamed.

"Isn't he cute?" she continued. The boys had to agree; the coati were awfully cute creatures.

They finished eating, and then continued upriver, passing through bright sun and thick shade, heading deeper into the wild.

Late in the afternoon, the channel opened into a broad lake dotted with cypress and willow and longleaf pine. Nose stopped rowing. Sawyer consulted the map. It showed a lake shaped like the contours of a gigantic catfish. A tiny circle within the fish shape may have indicated an island. Or an eye.

"Looks like this is where Moses ran into Ol' One Eye," said Sawyer. "We'll set some lines and camp here."

Truman unrolled a three-foot length of nylon leader from a spool. He took a king-size fishhook from a coffee can and tied it to the leader.

"Hook—" he called out, passing the hook to Nose. Nose sliced off a length of fishing line with his pocketknife and attached it to the hook and leader.

"Line—" Nose called out, and passed the line to Sawyer. Sawyer baited the hook with a slice of bacon, tied the line to a branch, and lowered the bait into the water.

"And—we sink 'er," finished Sawyer, taking up his oar.

"Wait," said Elvira.

She opened her Barbie lunch box, removed a glow-in-the-dark plastic star on a string, and draped it over a dead tree stump.

"What's that for?" asked Nose.

"A bright light," Elvira explained. "So we can find our way home in case we get lost. Like in 'Hansel and Gretel.'"

"This ain't no fairy tale, Virus," said Sawyer.

Elvira shrugged. "Better safe than sorry."

KERSPLASH!—the sound of a fish jumping came from somewhere behind them. As they turned, they saw that their wake was marked by dozens of lines already dangling from drooping branches and dead stumps.

"Looks like we're not the first ones to hunt Ol' One Eye on this lake," said Nose.

"But we may be the last," said Sawyer. "Moses said all of this will be flooded soon, because of the new dam."

They continued moving along the lakeshore, setting their lines.

As evening fell, a heavy stillness settled over the lake. The boys rowed while Elvira trained a flashlight along the bank, watching for those spots where a baited line bobbed in the water.

Her beam picked up a row of limp lines. Nothing yet. They oared past.

Darkness came swiftly among the trees. Truman pulled out a battery-operated lantern, turned it on low, and set it down in the bottom of the boat. Nose rummaged around for the mosquito repellant, and they all gave themselves a good smeary coating.

"Gettin' to be just about the right time of night for catchin' a big one," said Nose.

"You mean catfish are nocturnal?" asked Truman.

"Knock-what?" asked Elvira.

"Nocturnal," said Truman. "Means night-dwelling."

"You got it, Einstein," replied Nose. "Cats are creatures of the dark side. Night feeders."

Elvira's beam spotted a gently bobbing line. They rowed in close under a tree. Sawyer slowly pulled up the line. A small splashing fish broke the surface. He held it in the flashlight beam.

"Carp," announced Sawyer.

Nose gave a thumbs-down. Sawyer unhooked the fish and tossed it back into the water. The boys kept rowing. Elvira's flashlight roamed along the bank, picking up more dead lines dangling from trees. A rustling sound came from up ahead. Elvira's beam picked up another bobbing line. They rowed in close.

Again, Sawyer slowly pulled up the line. Another splashing fish broke the surface, bigger this time. Sawyer held it up in the soft light from the lantern.

"Catfish," announced Sawyer.

Nose gave a thumbs-up. "Dinner," he declared, unhooking the fish from Sawyer's line and depositing it in a cooler.

As night settled over the swamp, Sawyer kept checking their lines while Nose and Truman rowed and Elvira shined her light. They came up with a nice bass and a couple of sunfish and were discussing a break for dinner, when all at once they heard a thrashing and splashing from somewhere nearby. They paddled in the direction of the commotion. Elvira's beam revealed something. They all stopped and stared. The heavy willow branch on which they had tied their line was now bent low to the water. The taut line was moving in lazy circles. Something was caught on that line. Something big.

"Jeez—" whispered Nose.

"Far out—" said Truman.

"It's him—" said Elvira.

"Ol' One Eye—" finished Sawyer.

They rowed in closer. Sawyer grabbed the line and pulled. Whatever it was, it was yanking back.

"Little help here, guys," said Sawyer as he strained at the line. Truman didn't budge. Nose picked up an oar, wielding it like a weapon. Elvira aimed the flashlight.

"C'mon, what are we? Mice or men?" urged Sawyer.

Nose handed Truman the oar. He crowded behind Sawyer and grabbed hold of the line. They began to pull, hand over hand. Nose slipped, lost his grip, and banged into Elvira. The flashlight was knocked from her hand. It went out.

"Fix the light, Virus!" Sawyer said anxiously. Something was rising in the water, getting closer and closer. Elvira fumbled for the flashlight. She rapped it against her leg.

A large shape like an oversized turkey platter was breaking the surface. The four fishermen shouted and fell back as the thing was hauled into the boat. They all let go of the line and scrambled to the rear, shrieking.

The lantern in the bottom of the boat made it harder for them to see what lay in the shadows beyond. Then, suddenly, the creature lumbered forward and clamped its jaws down on the toe of Nose's sneaker.

It wasn't Ol' One Eye. It was a humongous—

"SNAPPING TURTLE!!!" they shouted.

Truman panicked. He started trying to row in reverse.

The willow branch, free of the turtle's weight, abruptly hauled back, yanking the terrapin clean out of the boat, with Nose's sneaker still in its mouth. The whiplash flung the reptile far across the water. The branch snapped. The turtle landed in the river with a huge splash.

"Now *that*'s a cannonball!" said Truman.

Elvira's flashlight came to life, and they spent the next twenty minutes searching for Nose's sneaker. They followed their fishing line from the willow and found that both the fish hook and the sneaker had been dislodged from the snapper's mouth when it was flung back into the lake, which was lucky for the poor turtle since it would not have had a happy life attached to that willow till the end of its days. The sneaker had landed among some cattails, and when Nose fished it out with an oar, he discovered a neat slice in the toe, which had barely missed his own.

Shortly after the turtle incident, Sawyer, Elvira, Nose, and Truman began to get very hungry. They had a fine catch on hand, so they decided to find a good spot along the lakeshore for a camp.

Before long, they were sprawled around a crackling fire. The freshly caught fish sizzled in a skillet, to be accompanied by roasted marshmallows, cheese puffs, and Yoo-hoos.

"My dad spent his whole life fishin' the Yazoo," said Sawyer, "and if there's anything he taught me, it's that there's only one way to catch the really big ones."

"I hate the really big ones," said Elvira.

"I hate the really little ones," said Nose.

"You don't fight the big ones," Sawyer went on. "You don't even let 'em know they're hooked. You give 'em their space. Let 'em feel they're home alone."

"Wish I were home," Truman complained. "First thing I'd do is drain my aquarium. Turn it into a terrarium."

"You gotta hold on quietlike," said Sawyer, ignoring Truman. He pantomimed as if he were fishing. "Till *juusst* the right time. Then, when they're least expecting it—" Sawyer yanked on his imaginary pole.

"Difference here," said Truman, "is y'all are the one's who are hooked—and you don't even know it."

Nobody could argue with that, and the group fell silent for a time.

"I bet Ol' Moses'd give anything to be here—" began Sawyer, when a terrible shriek shattered the stillness.

"What was that?" cried Elvira.

"Panther," said Sawyer, pretending not to be bothered.

"It—it sounded like—like someone screaming," said Truman.

"Nah. That don't come till later," said Nose. "When we carve you up for fish bait."

Nose licked his lips and made cartoonish "yum-yum" sounds. Truman swallowed hard. The others laughed nervously.

Beyond the campfire, the swamp came alive with the calls of countless nocturnal creatures, but they heard no more screams.

9

OL' TWO EYE

By THE TIME THEY FINISHED THEIR DINNER, IT WAS NEARLY midnight. A shimmering moon cleared the treetops as it rose over the misty lake.

Truman pumped out a discordant tune on his accordion. Elvira clapped while Sawyer and Nose just shook their heads.

Afterward, Truman and Elvira set about tidying up the camp and bringing water from the lake to drown the campfire. Sawyer and Nose made ready for the next phase of the hunt.

"Time to bring out the heavy artillery," declared Sawyer, when everyone was ready.

The boys piled into the boat, but Elvira had her eye on a fallen log that stuck out over the water. The weeping willow overhead was blocking the moonlight, and she thought that

Ol' One Eye might be hiding in the darkness right underneath that log.

"Me and Barbie are gonna fish from here," she called to the boys.

Sawyer opened up the small cooler, which had been reserved for the foul amalgamations the boys had made that morning. He baited his line with his peanut butter, dead frog, chewing tobacco, stuffed-in-a-bra-cup mess. Nose baited his line with his dog food, dead flies, motor oil, stuffed-in-a-rubber-chicken mess. Truman baited his line with his dead mouse, shaving cream, wrapped-in-a-slab-of-bloody-liver mess.

Elvira, her Barbie beside her, was seated on the log. She chewed up a baseball-sized gob of bubble gum, placed it on the log, and flattened it into a sheet. She rummaged in her lunch box. Out came a slice of chocolate cake, which she placed on the gum sheet and topped with some half-melted M&Ms. She found a tube of glitter and sprinkled some on, along with a splash of Kool-Aid from her thermos. She finished with some cheap perfume, dabbing herself and Barbie behind the ears before dousing her bait. She rolled the mess into a tight ball and sunk a hook in it.

She tossed her baited line into the water. It wasn't but a moment before her line tightened. "I got one—" she whispered. The line jerked hard, nearly yanking the pole out of her hands. "Haaallp! I got him!"

The boys in the boat looked over at her struggling. They

were not impressed. "Quit fooling around, Virus!" said Nose.

Another mighty jerk on the line yanked Elvira right off her log and into the shallow water. "I'm not! It's Ol' One Eye! He's big!"

The boys still thought she was playing a trick. After all, her line had been in the water for only a few seconds.

"Oh, yeah? How big?" Sawyer asked.

Another jerk on Elvira's line dragged her into waist-high water. "Biiiiiig!!!" she hollered.

The boys were starting to pay attention now, but they didn't want to be tricked by a little girl. "Bigger than Barbie?" Nose asked.

"Bigger than meeeeee!!!" Elvira yelled, the water coming up to her neck. "Haaaalllp!"

"Better check it out," decided Sawyer. He began rowing toward her.

Elvira strained to keep from going under. "Huuurrrryyyyyy! I can't hold on!"

They rowed alongside. Nose grabbed the pole. Sawyer and Truman hauled her into the boat.

"You believe me now?" she said.

Nose tested the line, but it had gone limp. "Virus, what'd your mom teach you about crying 'wolf' when there ain't even a flea-bitten, half-starved, mangy mutt—"

A huge shape leapt out of the water, sailed through the air, and landed with an awesome splash—it *was* a giant catfish! Nose was almost yanked overboard as Sawyer, Truman, and Elvira dove in to lend a hand.

• • •

Much later, the four fishermen lay slumped in the boat, tangled in fishing line; four pairs of blistered hands still clutched the pole. That monster cat had dragged them all over the lake. Ninety minutes and they still hadn't landed the giant fish. They felt like they'd fought through a war. But now the line trailed off into a narrow dead-end inlet. There was only one way out for the humongous cat. And they were blocking it.

"This is it, guys," said Sawyer, squaring his shoulders. "End game."

The others looked at him blankly. They were dog-tired, drained, and near done in.

"We've got him trapped; now all we gotta do is bring him in," Sawyer encouraged them. "Nose, where's that big net?"

Nose pointed to the seat under Truman.

"Get it," said Sawyer. "You three spread out behind me." He took the pole and climbed overboard into the knee-deep water.

"Hurry! Case he runs for it!" called Sawyer over his shoulder. The others perked up as they realized that the battle was almost over—and they just might win. Truman grabbed the net as they piled out of the boat.

The cat headed farther up the inlet.

Sawyer followed.

The others spread out, with Elvira in the middle.

Gripping the net between them, they sealed off the fish's escape route.

Sawyer's line grew taut as the fish bolted past, running for the lake. Sawyer lost his footing and belly flopped into the water. Still clutching the pole, he was dragged through the wake of that mighty fish and took in a lungful of water. He lost his grip on the pole, and it was wrenched from his raw and blistered hands.

The cat slammed into the net, plowing past Nose, Truman, and Elvira. The net stretched into a tight V as the fish made for open water. Sawyer stumbled up and they closed their trap. With their last remaining strength, they dragged the struggling cat to the bank. They all gathered around, sinking to their knees, thoroughly spent.

"What's our time, Tru?" asked Nose weakly. "They'll want it for the record books."

Truman checked his waterproof watch. "One hour, forty-two minutes, five seconds."

They stared at the gray torpedo flopping inside the net. It was a monster of a catfish, bigger than any they'd ever seen.

"It must weigh more than a hundred pounds!" exclaimed Nose.

The others nodded. Together they strained and hoisted the netted fish into a water-filled hollow in a fallen cypress.

"Now can we go home? Puleeze," whined Truman.

Nose draped an arm around Truman's shoulder. "Home? My man, this calls for some serious celebrating."

"Be more fun if we did it at home. Don't you think?" said Truman.

Nose ignored him and gestured at the giant cat. "We kicked some scaly butt, didn't we, Sawyer?"

"Catfish don't have scaly butts, you moron," said Elvira. "They don't even have scales."

Nose clapped Sawyer on the back. "We did it, Saw! We caught Ol' One Eye! Grandpa Moses spent his whole life chasing this giant cat. But we tracked him down in one day. Is he gonna be surprised or what?"

"Hey, let's go surprise him now!" said Truman. "Whatcha say? Come on, let's go home, surprise Mr. Moses. Huh?"

Nose hugged his two partners. "We're gonna be famous, guys. All three of us," he said.

Elvira held up her Barbie, shooting Nose a look. "Five of us," she said.

"Ah—right—five of us," said Nose, smiling begrudgingly at Elvira.

Sawyer waded into the murky water to check the lines securing the fish. "That should hold him," he said as he slogged back to the bank.

"Eeeewwww!" shrieked Elvira, pointing at Sawyer. A fat purple-black leech was clamped to his thigh.

"Whaa—what the heck is that?" stammered Truman.

"Leech," said Sawyer matter-of-factly.

"Big fat ugly one, too." Nose laughed.

"Gross!" said Elvira.

"Tru, get me those waterproof matches," said Nose.

"What for?" asked Truman.

"Watch and learn," said Nose.

Truman untied his matchbox from his accordion strap and brought it to Nose.

"Over on that log." Nose motioned to Sawyer.

Sawyer sat on the log while Nose struck a match. Elvira sat beside him.

"Ah, guys, you know," said Truman, taking a step back. "I was just thinking . . . somebody oughta gather more firewood . . ." He withdrew several more paces, but continued to watch.

Nose carefully positioned the match near the leech. "Be still now," he cautioned Sawyer. He held the flame close so that the leech could feel the heat, and soon enough it released its bite and dropped away.

"Nothin' to it," said Nose. He turned to Truman. "How 'bout that first aid kit?"

Truman retrieved the kit and handed it to Nose, who applied some antiseptic and a bandage to the small wound on Sawyer's leg.

"Thanks," said Sawyer. He returned to the lakeshore to gaze down at the great fish. Nose joined him, slapping Sawyer on the back again.

"Ain't that a sight," said Nose.

"I say we toss him back."

"Toss him—?" Nose looked around. "Did he say toss him? Someone pass me the Q-tips, my ears must be plugged. This here's the catch of the century. I want my mug on the front page of the *Belzoni Banner*, with Ol' One Eye here."

"Capital idea, Nose," said Truman. "Let's start back now. We can still make the Sunday paper. Come on."

Sawyer bent to the water-filled hollow, studying the fish. "I hate to ruin the party," he said, "but this ain't Ol' One Eye."

"What're you talking about?" said Nose. "That's the biggest cat I ever seen. It's gotta be him."

"Biggest cat I ever seen, too," said Sawyer. "But why do you think Moses called him Ol' One Eye?"

"'Cause he's only got—he's only got—" Nose hesitated. He had a sinking feeling that he knew where this conversation was going.

Elvira's hand shot up. She waved it in Sawyer's face. "I know. I know! 'Cause he's only got one eye?"

"Right," said Sawyer. "So that means Ol' One Eye is still out there somewhere."

They peered across the lake.

"Unlesssssss—" said Truman, hatching an idea, "—unless Mr. Moses was speaking metaphorically."

"That's just the word I was lookin' for," said Nose.

"Meta-wha—?" said Elvira.

"Explain it to them, Tru," said Nose loftily. "They ain't got the learnin' we got."

"A metaphor. Wise men like Mr. Moses use them all the time. They take any old word, then use it to mean something else. Kinda like a riddle; a mystery. You know, to make us think. Right, Nose?"

"Egg-zactly," agreed Nose. "You don't have to explain it to me, partner."

"Explain it to *me*, then," Sawyer said suspiciously.

"Well, pretend I'm a wise old man," said Truman. "Like Mr. Moses. I take the number 'one'—like in Ol' One Eye. Well, to the average Joe, like you guys—one means one. Right?"

"Duh," said Sawyer.

"But to the truly educated, 'one' is also the lowest cardinal number. And cardinals have how many eyes?"

Elvira waved her hand again. "Cardinals have two eyes."

"Right. So, knowing that, an educated person could easily make the logical connection that one means two. See? I've just made a metaphor." Truman smiled and looked around at his confused compatriots.

"Now wait a minute," said Sawyer. "You're saying—one equals two?"

"Metaphorically speaking, of course. So when Mr. Moses tells us to go and catch Ol' One Eye—he's really telling us to go catch Ol' Two Eye."

"Huh?" said Sawyer.

Nose slapped his new pal on the back. "Makes sense to me, Tru," he said. "And that there fish's got two eyes. So he's really Ol' One Eye, right?"

Truman shrugged smugly, pleased with himself for putting the matter to rest. "Of course. It's self-evident. Mr. Moses gave us a riddle. And we solved it." He looked at

Sawyer with a flicker of hope. "Uh, now that it's settled, can we go home?"

"You know, I feel so good I could go for a little of that accordion music right about now," said Nose.

Truman grinned. "Really? You could?"

"Heck, yeah. I'm no square. Let's go get that squawk box of yours, Tru, ol' buddy."

Nose threw an arm around Truman and led him back to their camp. Sawyer followed, shaking his head. Elvira trailed behind, thoroughly bewildered.

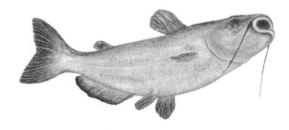

10

DREAMLAND

THE ANGLERS SPREAD THEIR SLEEPING BAGS AROUND THE damp ashes of the supper campfire and flopped down in exhaustion. They wolfed the last of their marshmallows cold and washed them down with tepid raspberry Kool-Aid. Truman lay back on his accordion, using it as a pillow. Elvira snuggled with her Barbie. Nose was already snoring.

Sawyer awakened in the dead of night. Nose was still snoring. Truman and Elvira slept soundly, Elvira still clutching her Barbie. He lay for a long time staring at the night sky chock-full of stars. Seven of the brightest stars formed the bowl and handle of the Big Dipper, which was part of the constellation Ursa Major, the Great Bear.

Sawyer knew a fair amount about the night sky because

his father had taught him. It was hard to actually picture a bear in that jumble of stars, but the Big Dipper was easy to spot.

He saw a shooting star, which he knew had nothing at all to do with stars, but was caused when tiny bits of rock and dust called meteoroids fell into the earth's atmosphere. He knew that after seeing one, he might see another, and when he did, he was ready with a wish about his mother and a golden ring and a monster cat. The isolated streaks of light became a shower, and he wished the same wish over and over and over.

Sawyer rose and looked down on his sleeping companions. It was good to have their company but from here on, he would continue alone. He carried his gear to the lakeshore, loaded the boat, and set forth. Keeping close to the shore, he soon entered the continuing weave of the Yazoo.

After rowing some distance, Sawyer began to hear soft rhythmic splashes in his wake. He looked back but saw no one. He supposed it could be a fish, but in his experience, fish didn't follow fishermen, not if they knew what was good for them.

Sawyer resumed rowing. Again he heard the sounds. He raised his oars and peered over his shoulder. The river was empty. He waited, but saw nothing. After navigating a bend, he angled into the shelter of a willow and waited to see who might come.

If it was a stranger, Sawyer would let him pass without

revealing himself. Then he heard more splashes and saw her oaring into view: Elvira, perched astride her Barbie lunch box. Only this was no ordinary lunch box; it was enormous, the little girl astride its humped back, oaring with a slab of driftwood. Sawyer maneuvered into the middle of the river to intercept her.

"Go back, Elvira." He didn't need to raise his voice. It carried easily in the stillness.

"I woke up and you weren't there."

"There's something I've got to do, and I don't want you part of it."

Elvira didn't respond. He turned his back on her and began to row. After a while he looked behind him and she was gone.

Ahead lay a fog bank. Sawyer rowed on and was soon enveloped. On and on he rowed until the mist grew thin and he emerged into the clear air, where he could once again see the river stretch before him in the pearly light. It was after the stars but before the sun, and he knew he had been rowing a long time.

The brown waterway remained, but the surrounding landscape had changed. Bamboo hedgerows framed green fields stretching away to distant gumdrop mountains. Groves of towering palms peppered the view between wetland crops where laborers bent to their tasks.

On the right bank, Sawyer made out a trio of large black animals with curving horns grazing in the shallows. They reminded him of the carved soapstone water buffalo teapot in the Brown family kitchen, a present sent home from his father. Sawyer knew he was no longer anywhere near Belzoni, no longer even in Mississippi; he was somehow in another world altogether.

The fields fell behind as the jungle took hold. Sawyer rowed on between dense walls of unfamiliar vegetation. He oared beneath a troop of snub-nosed monkeys cavorting in the canopy. He spied a thousand gaudy butterflies sipping moisture on a wet sandbar. He passed beneath a python, the biggest snake he had ever seen or could ever hope to imagine, lounging atop an overarching tree.

Rounding a bend, he came upon a metal military craft listing low in the river, her rusty deck awash with gently sloshing water. A black-necked crane took flight from the prow. A bobbing soldier's helmet clanked against a floating gas can. There was no sign of her crew.

The river bent again. Away to his left, a thick pillar of smoke stood against the sky above the palm line. As Sawyer drew near, he detected a faint odor, which reminded him of burning autumn leaves on the farm with his father. The light was fading again. As Sawyer rowed on, the scent grew stronger.

On the left bank, a thatched-hut village came into view, its bamboo and palm frond roofs ablaze with crackling orange fire. Pot-bellied pigs and pompous poultry wandered about in the smoky haze. Swirling ash ascended and dissolved into the darkened sky. A platoon of soldiers formed a bucket brigade between the river and the burning huts. Some were using wooden pails; others used their helmets.

Sawyer stared at the soldier nearest him, scooping water from the river. The soldier turned toward him, his face smudged with soot and smoke. Their eyes met.

"Dad! Dad!"

"Well, hey, Sawyer. You catchin' anything?"

"Dad—!"

"You're a long way from home, son."

"Mom got sick and I'm going to save her life."

"I'm proud of you. You're a good boy, Sawyer."

"I have to find her ring—it's lost—"

"Then I reckon you better keep searchin'."

"I'm trying, Dad, but—"

"You lookin' after your sister?"

"Yessir. She's here, too. With Truman and Nose." Sawyer pointed back downriver. "But I'm going on alone."

"There's some mighty big cats on this river."

"Was that your boat?" Sawyer asked.

His father nodded. "Guess I ran out of luck." Sawyer heard grief and regret in his father's voice. "I'm sorry I couldn't get back."

"Dad, I'm scared. I miss you." Sawyer could barely contain his tears.

"What are you afraid of?"

"I'm never going to see you again, am I?"

"I'm here now."

The other soldiers were gone. They had been swallowed

by billowing smoke. Only Sawyer's father remained. He spoke in a kind voice:

"I know you're afraid, but wherever you are, whatever you do, I'll always be close. Nothing is past. Nothing is ever lost. Try to remember that."

"Okay, Dad. I'll try."

The fires had mostly been doused or run out of fuel. Many of the huts had collapsed, leaving mounds of charred and smoldering remains.

His father spoke again, but his voice had grown thin and ghostly. Sawyer realized that his boat had begun to drift. One of his oars was missing.

"Dad!" he yelled. "Dad, I lost my oar—"

"I know you'll find it, Sawyer."

Smoke passed through his father like a gray river and then he, too, began to fade.

"Dad, no. Please! Don't go!"

"I'll always be here. This is my river now. The Yazoo is yours."

His father was gone, but his voice carried from the vanishing smoke.

"I love you, son."

Sawyer waited, but his father did not return.

"I love you, too—"

Sawyer awoke, damp with sweat, his heart thumping. He longed to return to the dream—to his father—but sleep would not come. He lay awake, listening to the steady breathing of his sleeping sister, cousin, and friend.

The night sky had grown cloudy while he slept, but he found a single star. It was not the best or the brightest star to wish upon, but it was the only one, and so he wished his wish again.

11

RED SKY IN MORNING

DAWN CREPT OVER THE GLASSY LAKE. CLOUDS GATHERED
in the east and were set ablaze by the red rim of the sun as
it broke the horizon.

The four companions were sacked out around the cold
remains of the campfire. Elvira was curled up near the dead
embers, and Sawyer had placed his sleeping bag between
her and the swamp.

Sawyer stirred. Quietly he rose and slipped away to the
lakeshore. He stared at Ol' Two Eye, lashed to the cypress.
He knew in his gut that Ol' One Eye was still out there—
somewhere.

He looked out over the lake. The low clouds, flaming
red, orange, and purple, were reflected in the mirror surface
of the lake. But Sawyer would've much preferred a plain
blue morning sky to this dazzling display.

The sound of footsteps made him turn. Elvira came alongside him and looked up at the sky.

"Red sky at night, sailors delight—" she began.

"Red sky in morning, sailors take warning," said Sawyer, finishing the old adage.

They stood for a moment, and then Elvira bent down to study the catfish.

"So—one and one is—four?" she asked.

"No. One and one is not four. One is one. And that ain't The One."

Elvira pointed at Ol' Two Eye, still confused. "He's the two—right?"

"No, no, no," Sawyer said. "Don't listen to them or you'll—oh, forget it." He sighed. "Yeah. He's the two. He's the two."

"Mom's gonna be so proud of us when she sees what we caught. This is really gonna make her happy."

"No, it's not."

"Why not?"

"Mom needs a miracle. And this ain't it. The miracle's out there somewhere. And I'm gonna find it. With or without those guys."

"Yeah. We don't need them."

"Look, Vi, if they're going back with Ol' Two Eye here, you're going back with them."

"No, I'm not. I'm—" but she stopped. Sawyer followed her wide-eyed gaze to the lake. The surface was smooth and calm, but a wave was rolling toward them. Fifty yards off. Picking up speed. Thirty. *Faster.* Twenty.

Instinctively, they stepped back. Ol' Two Eye seemed to sense a presence and thrashed weakly.

Ten yards. The wave kept coming. Sawyer pulled Elvira behind him. Five yards.

And then, the gaping, yard-wide snout of a monstrous albino catfish plowed up from underneath, swallowing Ol' Two Eye in one huge gulp, net and all.

Elvira screamed.

For a brief moment the line went taut, and then the rotting cypress crumbled and gave way. And just as quickly, that awesome mouth sunk back beneath the surface, and was gone.

Elvira and Sawyer stood stunned. "What was it, Sawyer?" she finally managed to blurt out.

"The miracle, Vi," Sawyer said. "That was the miracle."

Nose and Truman came running up. "Who screamed? What happened?" they asked, rubbing the sleep out of their eyes.

Sawyer pointed to the empty tree hollow. "Ol' One Eye," he said.

Nose looked at the hollow and then back at the lake. "You let him go? You let him go!"

"He came right outta that wave," Sawyer tried to explain. "He just swallowed that other—"

Nose leapt on Sawyer and wrestled him to the ground. They rolled about in the warm muck. "You're jealous!" Nose shouted. "You let him go because you didn't catch him yourself!"

Truman and Elvira tried to pull the two friends apart. "Guys! Guys! Can't we settle this—at home, maybe! Come on!" exclaimed Truman.

"Sawyer didn't do anything!" said Elvira. "Ol' One Eye ate Ol' Two Eye! I saw it! We both did!"

They managed to separate the two boys.

"Forget it, Vi," Sawyer said with disgust. "Talking to him," he said, pointing at Nose, "is like talking to—like talking to *him!*" He pointed at Truman.

Sawyer stormed back to their campsite.

Sawyer, Nose, Truman, and Elvira gathered their gear. Breakfast—the last of their bologna sandwiches—had been eaten in silence, Sawyer and Nose still fuming. More clouds gathered, and the air became as heavy as the mood among the foursome.

As they loaded their gear into the boat, Sawyer and Nose both grabbed hold of an oar at the same time. Truman and Elvira watched as the two stared each other down. At last, Sawyer relinquished the oar to Nose and gestured to a narrow channel winding off from the lake, snaking deeper into the swamp.

"He went thataway," Sawyer said.

12

SAILORS TAKE WARNING

All through the morning, as they rowed deeper into the swamp, the fiery low clouds of dawn built gradually into towering thunderheads of steel gray, and soon the first drops of rain began to fall. As the small craft headed into the wind, an ominous rumbling filled the air. A few minutes later, lightning flashed in the clouds up ahead.

"One-one-thousand, two-one-thousand, three—" counted Nose, before he was interrupted by the next rumbling.

"You know, there actually is a scientific explanation for that," said Truman. "The speed of sound is approximately one-fifth mile per second," he went on, "and, since it takes about one second to say the words 'one-one-thousand,' you're actually counting out the number of seconds between the flash of lightning and the thunder. Now, since light travels at one hundred and eighty-six thousand miles per second—"

Truman's lecture was interrupted by another flash of lightning, and this time they saw the jagged bolt striking toward the earth.

"One-one-thousand, two—" counted Nose, as a deafening roar pealed across the heavens. The storm was very near and, judging by the wind, headed straight for them. They exchanged anxious looks and continued to row.

Truman halfheartedly continued his speech about counting out the distance of a thunderstorm, but no one was listening and his voice soon trailed off.

Moments later, another bolt sprang from the furious sky and crashed into a tall tree off in the swamp. But the explosion of electricity and timber was drowned out by the earsplitting crack of thunder which ripped across the sky and was followed by tremendous crashing and booming, right overhead.

There was no need to keep counting. The storm was upon them. Wind lashed the little boat and drove the rain sideways as it sheeted from the leaden sky.

"We gotta find shelter!" shouted Truman.

"I know!" shouted Sawyer.

But for the past couple of hours, they had seen no dry land to speak of—only muddy, murky swamp. All they could do was keep rowing. Shivering, they pulled their extra clothing around them. Sawyer covered Elvira with his rain slicker, though it did little good. They were already drenched. They threw a tarp over their camping gear, but soon the boat would begin to fill and everything would be soaked.

Nose and Truman were on either side in the stern, each doing his best to scan port or starboard as he rowed. Elvira huddled in the middle, under Sawyer's raincoat. Sawyer was in the bow, scouting. His right hand was to his forehead, trying to keep some rain from his eyes. He blinked and shook his head to clear the rest.

Sawyer's father had taught him a lot about the outdoors, including about lightning. He knew it struck tall objects because they were closer; it struck water and metal because they were smooth conductors of electricity.

Sawyer turned to the others, his face grim. They were in a metal boat surrounded by water and tall trees. They were sitting ducks for a lightning strike. He turned back to his post.

At first, he thought it was just a trick of the mist and fog, but as he stared ahead, he saw that there was indeed some kind of structure back through the trees.

"Look," he hollered, pointing.

The others strained to see through the whipping rain. As they rowed closer, it appeared they were paddling up a broad avenue flanked by a double-row canopy of oaks. They realized they were approaching the sprawling remains of a long-decayed plantation home. Awestruck, they rowed closer.

What had once been a grand antebellum mansion was

now a dilapidated, flooded wreck. Moss-covered columns lined the sunken front porch and rotting upper veranda. Empty windows stared like eyes from its crumbling face. Louvered shutters hung askew. A dark passage formed a crooked mouth where wide front doors once stood.

The storm continued to lash at the boat as they made for the entrance. They oared past the thick round columns and floated inside.

13

THE LAIR

THEY DRIFTED INTO AN IMMENSE, DIM FOYER. SAWYER
pulled out a flashlight and played it around the moldy walls.
Slimy green algae spread over faded peeling wallpaper. A
sagging, curved staircase rose from the water. From the top
of the stairs, the banister continued around an upper-level
gallery, which formed a large U shape overlooking the foyer.
A once-fancy chandelier, now draped in a beard of Spanish
moss, swayed high above.

Nose whistled low.

"Far out!" said Truman.

"Wow!" said Elvira.

They rowed to the banister and secured the mooring
line.

"There's something about this place I don't like," said
Sawyer.

"It *is* creepy," agreed Truman.

"At least we're out of the rain," said Elvira.

"Let's try to get some rest," Sawyer said. They had gotten only a few hours of sleep the night before and might as well rest, if they could, while the storm blew itself out.

They unloaded the wettest gear and trudged up the slippery, wobbly stairs. Truman opened a warped door near the landing.

"Hey, look at this," he said.

They peered inside. A decaying four-poster bed dominated the dusty room, its tattered canopy as fragile as spider webbing. The room seemed fairly dry.

"Wow," breathed Elvira. She climbed on the bed and trampolined up and down, squealing and throwing up clouds of dust. The bed frame gave way, crashing the mattress to the floor.

"Oops," she said sheepishly, rolling off.

"There's enough room on that bed for all of us," said Sawyer.

"Think I'll sleep on the floor," said Nose, glowering at Sawyer. He still thought Sawyer had robbed them of fame and fortune by releasing Ol' Two Eye.

Elvira tugged at Sawyer's sleeve and whispered in his ear, "Barbie has to go."

"Jeez, Virus, not again."

"She can't help it."

"Okay, okay. You guys stay here," he said as he led Elvira out into the hall.

Truman turned to Nose. "I thought you and Sawyer were pals."

"*Were* is right, Einstein. Until he proved he's just like all the others."

"What others?"

"Go find a Belzoni phone book. Then go from A to Z. They're the others."

"What about your family?"

Nose scoffed. "I got eleven brothers and sisters, and there's only one or two who are ever gonna amount to duck doo. And I'm not one of 'em."

"Maybe you're on the runner-up list."

"You lookin' to mix?"

"No. What about your grandpa Moses?"

"Just 'cause he puts up with me doesn't mean he likes me."

"Well, I like you. You're the only pal I've got who appreciates good music. You taught me how to fish. You even know what a metaphor is."

"Hey, I'm not your pal, okay?" said Nose. "I don't need pals. All I need is to catch that cat. And get me some of that treasure. We'll see what they say 'bout Nose then."

Truman shrugged and stretched out on the bed, gazing up at the ceiling. "Know what I'm gonna do with my share? I'm gonna buy me an accordion with Swedish steel reeds. A black and silver one. With pearl inlay and real ivory keys. And it's gonna have my name spelled out in rhinestones."

Nose lay down on the bed. Dreams filled his head, too. "Gonna buy me a '49 Merc. Just like my old man's. But mine'll be better, 'cause it's gonna be chopped and channeled."

"Yeah, rhinestones," said Truman. He sighed. "But treasure won't make me a good enough musician to play in a real band. I get all nervous and clumsy just when I play in front of y'all."

"Chopped and channeled," echoed Nose. "And then I'm blowing this lousy swamp. When I'm rich and famous, all my 'pals' can eat my dust. All the way to Memphis."

"Hey, you can stay at my house. We can do crazy things together. Like play Parcheesi all night or maybe—"

"Cheese makes me sick. And you're starting to do the same."

"But I'm not like those others, Nose," said Truman.

"Only difference between you and them is they all think they're better than me—and you think you're better than them."

A loud bang came from down the hall.

"What was that?" asked Truman.

Nose grabbed a flashlight and moved to the doorway. "Sawyer—? Virus—?" he called softly. He motioned to Truman. "C'mon. They should've been back by now. Prob'ly got lost."

Nose and Truman crept down the hall. They came to a door on the right, slowly opened it, and saw another bedroom, empty except for the mildewed curtains still clinging to the window. They closed the door and went on down the hall. Another door. They peeked inside. They had found a back staircase.

"Must go down to the kitchen," said Nose. Truman nodded.

They heard the loud banging again. The gusting wind was slamming a door farther down the gallery. Nose and Truman approached cautiously. It was too dark to see inside. Nose flipped the switch on his flashlight, but it didn't come on. He rapped it against his leg as they entered the room.

BANG! The wind slammed the door shut behind them. Nose jumped and dropped the flashlight, which came on and fixed them in its beam, making the room around them darker still. They froze. An eerie bubbling sound came from a far corner.

"N-Nose—?" said Truman.

Nose stooped down, retrieved the flashlight, and pointed it ahead of them.

"AHHH!" shouted Truman.

He was face-to-face with a nightmare.

"Don't be such a fraidy-cat!" said Nose. "It's just a gator skull." He swiveled the light, revealing mounds of animal hides, pelts, and skulls. Black bear. Panther. Bobcat. Gator. Some were stacked, some hung by hooks. Scattered around the room were fishing nets and traps.

"Some serious poachin's going on here," said Nose. Sharp tools lay all around. Animal bones littered a chopping block and crunched under their feet.

The boys were drawn toward an enormous cauldron boiling over a gas flame. Truman shuddered. "Hey, Nose, remember what Elvira said about 'Hansel and Gretel'—?"

A towering figure eased from the shadows. Just then, lightning flashed outside the window, illuminating the looming form. Shaggy white hair framed a hooded face. Long bony fingers clutched at the boys just as thunder clapped.

"Helllllpp!" shrieked Nose and Truman. They struggled and broke free of the rangy grip and bolted for the door. Nose slipped on something slimy, lost his balance, and cracked his head against a table as he fell. He lay moaning—

The hooded figure cut Truman off at the door as another bolt of lightning highlighted its hideous face. Truman screamed and leapt up on the chopping block.

"Nose! Nose!" he shouted desperately as the figure grabbed at him. Truman scampered up a pile of gator hides, toward an opening in the cracked ceiling. There was nothing he could do for Nose now, except go for help. He hauled himself into the crawl space, kicked free from the grasping hand, and disappeared.

Nose shook his head groggily and looked up. The ghastly being reached for him.

When Sawyer and Elvira returned to the bedroom, there was no sign of Nose or Truman.

"Rats!" said Sawyer. "I told them to wait."

He and Elvira stepped back into the hall and moved down the long, dark corridor. Sawyer was just about to say something when—

CRASH! An object exploded through the ceiling. They jumped back as it dropped in a heap at their feet, then took shape and grabbed at them. Sawyer and Elvira yelped in terror.

But it was only Truman. He'd fallen through the rotting crawl space into the hall.

"We don't have time for games, Tru," grumbled Sawyer, recovering his wits.

"A w-witch!" Truman gasped, eyes bulging. "A witch got him!"

"A witch? What're you talking about?"

"A witch!" Truman croaked, still trying to catch his breath. "All dressed in black—long white hair—fangs this long—ugliest thing I've ever seen—she had this pot—bubbling over with dead stuff—she's gonna cook Nose—she's gonna cook all of us—"

"Make him stop, Sawyer," whimpered Elvira. "He's scaring Barbie."

"No such thing as a witch, Tru. Calm down, okay?" Sawyer led them back toward the bedroom at the top of the stairs.

In a rush, Truman told them what had happened in the room at the end of the hall, and how he had narrowly escaped. "We've got to save Nose!" he said.

• • •

The cadaverous figure—shrouded in a cape of scraggly animal hides—grasped Nose's arm with a bony hand and shoved him into a chair. It leaned in close. Nose could see its ruined teeth.

Nose gasped as he glimpsed the face beneath the drooping hood. It was horribly scarred all over one side, from the crooked mouth to the milky eye.

It was a terrifying presence, but, Nose realized, it was not a witch. Ugly, nasty, and no doubt mean—but the vile visage was most assuredly that of a man. And that man, Nose now understood, was a poacher.

This knowledge, however, did not provide poor Nose with any sense of relief; on the contrary, a deepening sense of dread was sinking into his bones.

Nose had been warned about the dangers of the swamp for as long as he could remember. A kid could get lost out here and never find his way home. He could get eaten by gators, or drown, or starve before anyone would find him. There were bobcats and panthers, poisonous snakes, quicksand, and all manner of other dangers, not the least of which were poachers.

Poachers were outlaws, and they weren't likely to want their hideouts uncovered or their livelihoods jeopardized. And now, Nose was face-to-face with one of them. How far would a poacher go to keep his secrets?

Well, we're in it now, thought Nose. He knew he ought to be scared, but he just felt mad.

He was mad at Sawyer for letting Ol' Two Eye go, and mad at Truman for escaping while he had gotten caught. He was mad about losing his favorite hat, and getting a hole in the toe of his brand-new sneakers, for which, he was sure, he would catch three kinds of heck from his mom when he got home. *If* he got home.

And now this creepy criminal—who, instead of threatening kids, should be locked in a cell at the state penitentiary—was shaking a gruesome instrument in his face. Nose didn't want to guess what it appeared to be crusted with.

"What're you runts doin' way ou'chere?" the poacher demanded, as he turned and spat a spray of tobacco juice on the filthy floor.

"Fishin'. Just catfishin'," Nose said defiantly.

"Last chance, gator bait, or how's 'bout I reach up that big sniffer a'yers and drag yer brains right out, like I done to all them critters there," the poacher said, brandishing the wicked-looking instrument. "You got t'at?"

Nose wondered if the old man was putting him on. He opened his mouth, then hesitated.

"Spit it out, boy. I ain't in no mood for games." The poacher poked Nose's chin with the sharp tool.

"We're looking for Ol' One Eye," Nose said, staring into the hideous face with the cloudy left eye.

"You found 'im," the poacher said, leaning closer. "Too bad fer you."

Nose stared straight into the poacher's good right eye. "Nuh-uh," he said boldly. "Ol' One Eye's bigger 'an you. And prob'ly meaner, too."

"Mighty big talk fer a li'l feller I'm fixin' ta skin like a snake."

Nose tried to think. If he could get the poacher out of the room and into the hall, his friends might be able to help. He had an idea.

"Don't really care much about the fish," he said. "It's the treasure I got a nose for."

"Treasure, huh? Ya 'spect me ta believe that, boy?"

"The name's Nose."

"Well, *Nose*," sneered the poacher, jabbing him again, "suppose ya tell me what's with this treasure."

"We got a map. Back up the hall."

"S'at so?" The poacher fixed his good eye on Nose and raised his eyebrow.

"Th-that's if my buddy didn't already take off with it," added Nose.

"Bad luck fer you iffin he done." The poacher sunk his claws into Nose's shoulder, pulled him out of the chair, and shoved him toward the door.

BANG! Sawyer, Elvira, and Truman turned as a door slammed open down the hall. They crouched in the bedroom doorway as the poacher shoved Nose into view at the far end of the gallery. A flash of lightning silhouetted the poacher's long silver hair and billowing poncho.

"Witch!" gasped Elvira.

"Told you," Truman whispered.

"Hush," Sawyer rasped. "If we're gonna help Nose, we can't get caught, too. Come on."

They slipped away to the staircase and eased into the shadows. From there, they watched as the poacher prodded Nose up the hall toward the bedroom, where their gear— including the map—was laid out to dry.

Sawyer gestured for Elvira and Truman to follow him down the creaking stairs to their boat. They huddled at the bottom, watching Nose and the poacher enter the bedroom above. The poacher glanced up and down the hall and then kicked the door shut.

"Listen," Sawyer whispered. "That's no witch. Looks to me like we're holed up in a poacher's lair."

"We've gotta get Nose and get the heck out of here," said Truman.

Sawyer nodded and turned to Elvira. "You wait in the boat, Vi," he said. "Soon as you see us coming, you cast off quick. Can you handle that?"

"Please don't leave me here alone, Sawyer."

"You're not alone. You've got Barbie with you."

Elvira looked at her battered Barbie. "Well, yeah, but—"

Sawyer spoke in a Barbie voice: "Oh, we'll be okay,

Sawyer. Me and Elvira can catch some supper while you're gone."

"Great idea, Barbie," said Sawyer in his normal voice. "Here, you and Vi take this pole. Maybe you'll snag another big one."

Elvira perked up at this. Sawyer was giving her credit for hooking Ol' Two Eye. "Maybe bigger!" she said, accepting the fishing pole.

Sawyer grabbed a net from the boat and turned to his cousin. "Okay, Tru, here's the plan. . . ."

14

HOOKED

THE POACHER BENT OVER THE MAP, WHICH HE HAD SPREAD on the broken bed. Nose was inching toward the door, ready to make a break for it, when they were startled by a plaintive moaning.

Yanking Nose toward the door, the poacher opened it a crack and peered into the hall. "What'n tarnation's 'at?" He scowled. The harrowing wail was drifting from the far end of the dim corridor.

Down in the boat, Elvira baited her hook as Sawyer had suggested. *This is no time for fishing*, she thought, but it gave her something to do while she waited. Keeping one eye on the closed door at the top of the stairs, she tied the fishing line to a cleat on the bow. Then she made ready to cast off, untying the mooring rope from the banister, looping it once, and holding on to the loose end.

The door upstairs burst open, and Elvira could just make out Nose being pushed into the hall again. She scrunched down, even though it was probably too dark for them to see her.

She heard a sound and turned toward the front entrance to see a half-drowned, chittering coatimundi paddling up the tree-lined avenue. The critter swam into the foyer and looked around with frightened eyes.

If the poacher heard the noises and looked down, he might see her. Silently, she willed the animal to be quiet. To her great relief, the coati paddled away through a double doorway into an adjoining room.

Just as the creature moved out of sight, Elvira felt a wave beneath the boat, lifting the small craft and setting it back down.

"Whoa," she whispered, scanning all around. But there was nothing to be seen except the dark water.

The coatimundi paddled frantically through the flooded dining room, searching for a place to hide. It swam toward another door, found it open just a sliver, and squeezed through. It had entered a long, narrow room which had once been a butler's pantry but was now nothing more than a dead end. The coati scampered to a high counter, squeaking nervously, its eyes glued to the door—a door that now slowly began to open—

Something was forcing that door—something under

the water. A massive white shape, barely visible beneath the murky surface, eased into the small room, filling it completely.

The coati watched in terror as a gaping mouth rimmed with yard-long barbells broke the surface. The thrash of a mighty tail slammed the door shut, sealing the monster cat and the coati inside. The beast tried to turn around, but it was too big. It was stuck!

Upstairs, the poacher, his good eye darting furtively, prodded Nose along in front of him. Outside, the storm continued to rage. Lightning illuminated the walls in jerky flashes while thunder cracked and boomed. The moaning sounds grew louder.

Down in the pantry, the titanic cat had become infuriated by his predicament. He had not lived this long—escaped a thousand hooks and traps—only to meet his end in a closet! He swung from side to side, slamming his mammoth bulk against the pantry wall. WHAM! The mansion trembled. Plaster crumbled; cracks raced up the wall and across the ceiling.

"What'n the heck's goin' on 'round here?" demanded the poacher.

"Earthquake?" said Nose. He had a fair idea what the weird moaning might be, but the quaking house was getting him pretty spooked.

SLAM! The fish battered the wall again.

Elvira trembled in her boat.

Nose and the poacher hesitated as the floor wobbled underfoot.

The eerie moaning grew louder.

At the far end of the hall, Truman hid behind a door. He'd gotten so carried away with pumping his accordion that he hadn't noticed how everything was shaking. But now he stopped as he saw a crack opening up in the floor.

Meanwhile, Sawyer had concealed himself in the crawl space above the ceiling where Truman had fallen through. He crouched over the opening with the fishing net, waiting for Truman's weird noises to lure the poacher underneath.

Another tremor shook the mansion. The crack widened in the floor near Truman. Lightning revealed a furry paw groping through the fracture. Truman's eyes popped wide as the screeching creature began to crawl through. He bolted from behind the door, squashing more wails from his accordion as he fled.

Nose and the poacher had just started down the hall, when—WHAM!—the mansion shuddered again. At that very moment, they passed beneath Sawyer's hiding place, and the trap was sprung. Sawyer dropped and landed on the poacher's shoulders, covering him with the net. The outlaw sprawled forward, yelling and windmilling his net-covered arms. Sawyer tumbled out of the way as Truman burst onto the gallery and tore down the hall, still pumping his accordion. A small, furry creature appeared to be chasing him.

The poacher stumbled into a doorway, bellowing and cursing as he tried to untangle himself. Truman ran pell-mell into Sawyer and Nose, and they all went down in a heap. The coati raced past.

Another great boom shook the house. The coati streaked down the stairs, leapt into the water, and paddled furiously out the front doorway.

Elvira hardly noticed. Her eyes were riveted on the corridor above. A vertical crack snaked up the wall, and even as she screamed a warning, the entire gallery began to give way.

The poacher, separated from the boys by the crumbling floor, threw himself through the doorway where he was crouched.

KABOOOOMMM! With a final lunge, the enraged fish breached the wall and whooshed back into the dining room.

Elvira, quaking in her boat, watched, transfixed by the drama unfolding above.

The boys struggled to their feet as the corridor collapsed beneath them. The railing lining the gallery had fallen away, and now Sawyer leapt out over the foyer, grabbing hold of the chandelier in midair. He swung by his arms. "Guys! Jump!" he yelled, raising himself to get a foothold on the chandelier.

Truman and Nose flew down the hall. Truman made it to the top of the staircase; he grabbed the banister and hung on. Nose was right behind him. He reached for the banister—but it was too late. The gallery crumbled, and he was hurled down into the dark water beneath an avalanche of debris.

"Nose! Nose!" they all shouted.

Sawyer was dangling right above Nose. He couldn't let go and risk landing on him.

Truman turned and launched himself in a daredevil leap from the top of the stairs. He cleared the debris and splashed into the water, searching desperately.

"Nose! Nose!" he called.

Sawyer looked around. What could he do? If he could just get to the staircase—

Truman took a deep breath and dove under the water.

"Sawyer!" Elvira screamed. "Do something!"

Sawyer was already swinging his legs. The chandelier began to sway, slowly at first, then gaining momentum. Sawyer's eyes were fixed on the staircase.

Truman broke the surface, gasping for air. He inhaled in gulps and dove back under. Elvira gripped the sides of the boat, but she could only watch helplessly.

Sawyer swung the chandelier faster now. Just as he was making a carefully timed leap for the staircase, Truman broke the surface again, this time hauling a barely conscious Nose. He unstrapped his accordion and blew into the bellows. Using it as a float, Truman draped Nose's arms over it and began dragging him toward the boat.

Sawyer had made it to the staircase, where he now hung from the banister, watching the rescue below. Elvira dropped the mooring line, grabbed an oar, and extended it toward Truman.

Sawyer was climbing onto the staircase when something caught his eye. The storm had let up, and a beam of sunlight shafted through the front doorway. In the sunlit water, he saw the massive, pale shape of an albino catfish plowing into the foyer, pushing a frothy wave in front of him.

"Ol' One Eye!!" shouted Sawyer.

Elvira turned as the swell swept under the boat, pitching her from side to side. She tumbled over the seat board, and the oar clattered back into the boat.

Truman and Nose were still in the water. Nose was wide awake now, awestruck at the sight of the mythic catfish.

KABLAM! A shotgun blast reverberated through the mansion. The poacher was standing in a dilapidated pirogue. He had made it to the rear staircase and must've had the wooden boat tied up in the kitchen. He had push-poled through the dining room and appeared in the doorway to the foyer. His first shot at the beast had missed, and he was aiming for a second.

Ol' One Eye veered and headed straight for the pirogue. The fish swept underneath, pushing a surge of water and tipping the boat. The poacher lost his balance and flipped overboard. The shotgun exploded, missing its intended target and blowing a hole in the ceiling instead.

A wrenching sound split the air. The foundation beams overhead began to crumble. A crack opened above the poacher, and his treasures rained down upon him. Gator hides. Animal pelts. Fishing nets. Traps.

"Noooooo!" he wailed.

In the next instant, Elvira's boat jerked forward. Ol' One Eye, despite having been shot at twice, had stopped for a snack on his way out! He had swallowed her bacon-baited hook, which she had secured to the bow. She lunged for the mooring rope, but it was yanked from her hands. With a sick feeling, she watched the loose line whip around the banister and trail in the water. She turned. The giant catfish was indeed towing her.

And that cat was angling straight for the front doorway.

She locked eyes with her brother, who was bounding down the collapsing stairs. "Sawyer!" she screamed. He reached the water and made a leap for the boat, but it was too far. Elvira held an oar out to him, but Ol' One Eye was already out the doorway, towing her boat in his wake.

Sawyer turned and splashed toward the empty pirogue. He hauled himself in and quickly push-poled toward Truman and Nose, dragging them aboard. Truman loaded his waterlogged accordion. They poled toward the doorway as fast as they could, leaving the poacher floundering and cursing his luck as he tried to save his hides, pelts, nets, and traps.

• • •

Ol' One Eye towed Elvira up the flooded, tree-lined avenue. His broad back and dorsal fin were visible above the surface.

"Haaaalllp!!!" she screamed.

The boys push-poled the poacher's leaky pirogue as fast as they could. Ol' One Eye veered off, towing Elvira across a shallow lake that covered the plantation grounds. Away in the distance, she saw what looked like a wrought iron fence. Maybe that would slow Ol' One Eye down. "Huurrryyy!!!" she screamed, turning toward the boys.

The rowboat banged up against something. Elvira gasped. The fish was towing her through a graveyard! It must have been the burial ground for the plantation family. Ol' One Eye was scraping past the partially submerged crypts and tombstones.

The boys were falling fast behind. Ol' One Eye wove between the tombstones, heading for the entrance of a large crypt. As the fish plowed through the dark interior, Elvira's long, sustained scream echoed off the dank and musty walls. Twin rows of crumbling caskets passed in a blur. The huge fish easily plowed through the rear wall and wove on.

The boys followed. Without warning, a moldy, grinning skeleton reared up from the tomb and slumped toward the pirogue as if it were reaching for the boys. Shrieking, they beat it back with their poles.

Ol' One Eye headed for the fence enclosing the graveyard. Elvira held her breath, but the giant cat plowed his way through, entirely unfazed by the obstacle.

The boys poled through the gap. Ol' One Eye angled into a shallow channel and took off at high speed.

The boys strained to keep up. Elvira's boat grew smaller and smaller. Ol' One Eye veered into another channel and kept going. He was aiming for the narrow space between a pair of trees. To Elvira it looked like threading a needle. She clutched her Barbie and braced herself for a titanic wipeout.

"Saawyerr!" she yelled. But the boat somehow scraped between the tree trunks and kept moving.

Sawyer cupped his hands to his mouth and hollered, "Juummp—Elviiraahh—juuummmp!" But she was either too far away to hear or too scared to leap out. The boys reached the passage and poled between the cypress trunks, but it was no use. Elvira's boat was just a toy craft in the distance.

And then it was gone.

Sawyer stopped poling. They stared all around. Steaming swamp stretched in every direction. Elvira had vanished. And they were lost.

"Where's the map?" asked Truman. They looked at each other.

Sawyer knew it was all his fault. If only he hadn't made Elvira stay by herself in the boat! She hadn't wanted to. Why did he have to tell her to fish while she waited? He could've had her wait at the bottom of the stairs, he could've—

Sawyer sighed and shook his head. "I've got to find her," he said. "I've got to—"

"We'll help you," said Truman, putting a hand on Sawyer's shoulder.

Nose nodded. "We'll find 'er, Saw," he said.

The boys looked around again. A clammy blanket of fog had settled over the swamp. Tall cypresses rose from the mist. They were adrift in a gray world where air and water seemed as one, like floating in a dream.

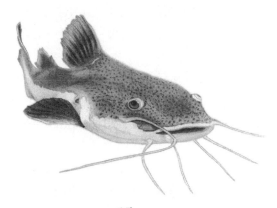

15

GATOR BAIT

SAWYER PONDERED THEIR SITUATION WITH GROWING frustration. How had he let things get into such a mess? Elvira, alone in the swamp—and here he was, stuck in a stupid leaky pirogue, and not so much as a thimble to bail with. He yanked off his sneaker and began shoveling shoefuls of water over the side.

Truman matched Sawyer's example and began to bail. "We've gotta go back for help," Truman told him gently. "We'll never find her on our own, Sawyer."

Sawyer shook his head. "By the time we get back to Belzoni, this'll all be one big lake," he reminded them. "We gotta keep going."

Nose also pulled off a shoe and began to scoop water out of the boat. He made a sweeping gesture. "Going where? We're lost."

"DO YOU THINK I'M GOING TO LEAVE MY SISTER OUT HERE FOR—FOR GATOR BAIT?" Sawyer yelled.

"'Course not, Saw," Nose said quickly. "We're as worried 'bout her as you are. But be realistic. What chance do we have out here with no food, no supplies—we're as lost as she is."

"Well, not exactly," said Truman. "Some of the gear was still in her boat—the cooler, some fishing gear—she'll have food at least—" He didn't meet Sawyer's eyes as he added, "That is, if she's still with the boat—"

"'Course she's with the boat!" said Nose, shooting Truman a reproachful look.

"What's the point of turning around?" Sawyer said. "We could never find our way back the way we came. We've gotta keep moving." He didn't wait for their agreement, but turned and laid into his pole.

They poled along in silence until Sawyer stopped. Nose and Truman stopped, too.

"What's up, Saw?" asked Nose.

"I've been thinking—" said Sawyer. "The Yazoo goes upriver to the northeast from Belzoni, right?"

Truman and Nose shrugged.

"So that means we were headed northeast all day yesterday." He looked expectantly at the boys, and they shrugged again.

"Now, when we got up this morning at Catfish Lake, the sun was rising over the far end where we camped—right near where we trapped Ol' Two Eye in the inlet—the east end—you see? That means, when we took the channel off to the right—that means we set out heading south."

"Whatcha gettin' at, Saw?" said Nose.

"Pay attention!" said Sawyer. "Once it got cloudy this morning, I don't know which way we were going, and the sun would've been too high to tell anyway. But look where the sun is now."

Although the late afternoon was gray and misty, they could still see the orange glow of the sun heading toward the western horizon. The sun was setting somewhere between due left and straight ahead.

Truman snapped his fingers and pointed at Sawyer. "Northwest," he said, "we're heading northwest."

Nose cocked his head. "Wait a minute—" he drawled, "wait—a—minute! You mean—you're thinking we've made a giant circle?"

"Well, I can't be sure, but I think—if we keep heading the way we've been going, we just might be able to find Elvira, and maybe find Ol' One Eye, and find our way back home, and maybe find the ring, too."

"Ring? What ring?" Nose said.

"Uh, I meant, uh, the treasure," said Sawyer.

"C'mon, give," demanded Truman.

"Yeah, 'fess up," said Nose.

"Okay, okay. It's—it's my mom's wedding ring," Sawyer admitted. "Ol' One Eye has it."

"WHAT? That's a good one." Nose snorted. "We're all

gonna die out here 'cause you took us on a scavenger hunt lookin' for a ring your mom lost?"

"Couldn't you have just bought her a new one?" asked Truman.

"A new one won't save her life. This one might."

"Get real," said Nose. "That darn ring already cost you a sister. And it ain't gonna save your mom's life neither. The doctors are gonna do that."

Sawyer glared at Nose. "You don't know. My dad gave her that ring, and Mom was always happy when she was wearing it. Like some part of him was still with us. Watching over us. I never thought about it till she lost it."

"That's about the dumbest thing I ever heard," said Nose.

"I don't know," said Truman. "My grandma wears a brass bracelet for her arthritis. And it works. Maybe that ring works the same way."

"If I'd known this fishing trip was gonna turn into a snipe hunt, I'd've stayed home," said Nose.

"No, you wouldn't've. You'd still be here," said Sawyer.

"No fish and no ring is worth dyin' for."

"We both know why you came, Nose."

"I don't know what you're talking about."

"You're no good as a sniffer, that's why. Not since you caught that ball with your face. You know you'll never fill your family's shoes at the plant. You're here 'cause you're trying to do something no one's ever been able to do before. So you can show the whole world you're not a total loser."

Nose glared at Sawyer.

"So? What's wrong with that?" asked Truman. "No one likes being a total loser."

"Yeah. What's wrong with that?" said Nose.

"Nothing. There's nothing wrong with that," replied Sawyer. "I'd do the same myself. And I'd hope my buddies would lend a hand."

Truman raised his fist. "Right on. I'll help you. We're a team, aren't we?"

Sawyer and Nose continued to stare each other down. "All I know is I came out here to catch a giant fish. Not go trawlin' for rings," said Nose.

"But it's the *same* thing, the fish and the ring. We catch Ol' One Eye, we might find the ring. In his nest. With the rest of the treasure," said Sawyer.

"But what about Elvira?" said Truman.

"She's with Ol' One Eye," Sawyer said.

"You really believe that?" asked Nose.

"I don't have much choice. I gotta believe."

"Man, we've got a lot of believing to do, don't we?" said Truman.

As dusk fell in the bottomland, the boys were pulling the pirogue up on a tiny island. Hours of fruitless searching had left them exhausted and dejected. They tumbled out and slumped on the clammy ground: wet, cold, hungry, thirsty, and all around miserable.

"I guess you guys know that Yazoo means River of

Death," said Truman. "Think I finally figured out why."

Nose kicked at the old boat. "We need a break," he said.

"Alright," said Sawyer. "But we start searching again at moonrise."

One by one they dozed off into a fitful sleep filled with nightmares of a missing girl, a gaping mouth, and water, water, water. The moon rose through the clouds, but the boys did not wake.

Far into the night, Nose stirred and sat up groggily. Sleeping on the damp ground had left him stiff and sore all over. He groaned and stared off into the swamp where clouds scudding past the moon revealed a patch of dim light.

"Uh-oh," he breathed.

A pair of green orbs were glowing from the black tree line.

"Pssst. Ah, guys," Nose whispered. "Better wake up."

Sawyer and Truman stirred and rubbed their eyes. They peered off into the darkness where Nose pointed. "That poacher—must've tracked us down," said Sawyer.

Shafting moonlight fell on the surrounding trees. They now saw a pair of yellow globes join the green ones. Alarm bells clanged in their heads.

"Oh, man," said Nose, "those ain't human. Them's gator eyes."

The last of the storm clouds broke, revealing a nearly full moon, which bathed the little island in shimmering light.

The boys realized that eyes were glowing from all around the bayou.

"It's over—we're surrounded!" Nose croaked. He reached in his pocket and pulled out his jackknife.

Sawyer turned to Nose. "Give me your knife."

"No way. Every man for himself."

"Give," insisted Sawyer, extending his hand.

Nose reluctantly turned over his knife. Sawyer slogged off in the waist-high water.

"Hey, are you crazy?" called Truman as Sawyer waded toward the tree line.

Nose and Truman looked around for something to arm themselves.

"Push poles," said Nose, grabbing one from the boat.

"Where's the other one?" said Truman, splashing around. "Where is it?"

"Never mind," said Nose, motioning to Truman to grab the other end of his pole.

Together they bent the pole around a stump until it snapped in two, then stood back-to-back, covering each other against the impending attack.

Off in the darkness, Sawyer stopped in front of a tree. Nose and Truman waited nervously, wielding their makeshift weapons.

"Bad time to be carving your initials," called Nose.

Sawyer slogged back toward the island. "Here's your gator eye," he said. He handed one of the shining "eyes" to Nose. It was a plastic glow-in-the-dark Saturn, one of Elvira's baubles.

"Way to go, Vi," said Nose, grinning in relief.

They quickly fashioned more push poles, using Nose's jackknife on several saplings. Then they set off, poling through the misty, moonlit bayou, stopping only to bail with their shoes.

16

MULBERRY SNOW

Truman heard the caw of a bird. As he looked up, a splat of white glop landed right between his eyes and rolled down the bridge of his nose. He'd just been bombed with a spoonful of mulberry-laden bird poop.

Each lost in his thoughts, the boys had failed to notice that the water was littered with white, thumb-sized berries. They had poled beneath a wild mulberry tree.

The tree must have been thirty feet high, its lower branches out of reach. One of them would have to climb. Sawyer plucked a slender reed and snapped it into three pieces. He offered his clenched fist to Nose and Truman. After considerable bellyaching about drawing the short straw, Nose climbed into the lower branches and gave them a good shake, producing a shower of fat berries.

Watching the falling white fruit from his perch, Nose

was reminded of the only time he had ever seen real snow. It was the day before Christmas, the year before last. The family was making a car trip to visit his father, who was serving a sentence at the Mississippi State Penitentiary, also known as Parchman Farm.

Nose had too many brothers and sisters to fit in the car, but he was among those who were old enough to go. Their mother was in bed with the flu, so Grandpa Moses drove. They were delivering a Christmas present: a new pair of shoes.

The morning was bleak and chilly as they set out. By the time they reached Sunflower County, it had begun to snow.

Moses said it reminded him of the thin white blanket that had descended on the Delta when he was just a boy. He had built a snowfish. It was his first attempt at a sculpture, and only lasted a couple of hours before it melted, but he was hooked.

Nose liked the snowfish story, but a question weighed heavily on his mind.

"Grandpa Moses, why can't Pa come home for Christmas?" he asked.

Moses chose his words carefully.

"Well, son, your daddy got into some trouble. He got himself mixed up with a sorry sort."

They drove for some miles before Nose spoke again.

"But why—why would he do it?"

Moses hesitated. "It ain't no easy thing, raising a bunch

of young 'uns," he said. "Family responsibilities can weigh heavy on a man."

Nose frowned, wondering if there was more to it than his grandpa was telling.

"Your daddy, he thought he saw a way to make some extra money," Moses continued. "Money that could've made things easier for your ma and you kids. That kind of temptation is a powerful thing."

The children had grown quiet as their grandpa spoke on a subject that their mother didn't allow discussed in the house.

"Your daddy made a mistake, and he has to face the consequences. That means not being able to be with his family right now, which is where he wants to be more than anywhere else."

"Will he be home for Christmas next year?" This time the question came from Nose's older sister Ivy.

"Yes, yes he will, and if I know my son, I expect he'll be home every Christmas from now on," Moses assured them.

The prison entrance was bedecked in holiday lights, as were the hedges lining the long road to the main building. But the family was stopped at the gate. There had been a mistake; the prisoner named Malcolm Adams wasn't available for their scheduled visit. He was out somewhere on a work detail.

When they left the grounds, they took a wrong turn and got lost in a maze of back roads. The landscape was dressed in a thin coat of speckled white.

Grandpa Moses hesitated at a stop sign. "This'll be south," he said, turning left.

Up ahead they saw a group of men. It was the work detail from the prison. Inmates were shoveling dirt from a dump truck, filling a roadside ditch. They were watched by guards on horseback who carried long rifles.

Moses slowed, and Nose thought he recognized his father among the stooped men. He pressed his face to the cold window and shouted, "Dad!" One of the men straightened and looked after the passing car.

Nose rolled down the window. "Dad!" he yelled again. His siblings had to stop him from climbing out and tumbling into the road. They yanked him back, but not before he was able to toss the boxed gift. After hitting the tarmac, it bounced into a ditch. The last thing Nose saw was a guard riding up to the box. He called over one of the prisoners and motioned him to hand it up.

After that day, Nose had a recurring dream of mounted guards coming to get him. Whenever he was tempted toward trouble, the memory of that day, and of the dream, made him think twice.

Nose climbed down from the tree and sat in the pirogue with his friends, gobbling the mulberry snow.

Truman was wishing he had a bottle so that if things didn't work out he might write a final farewell to his family. He would place his note in the bottle and cork it, then set it adrift in the hope it might someday be found. He had once read a book by the famous French oceanographer Jacques Cousteau, in which the author, reflecting on a harrowing journey to uncharted reaches of the Amazon, had compiled a series of lists. Truman composed his own mental lists:

THINGS I HAVE LOST

1 PAIR GOGGLES
1 PAIR FLIPPERS
1 SNORKEL
2 PAIR SOCKS
1 PAIR CUTOFFS
1 CAN SUNSCREEN
1 CAN BUG REPELLENT
1 FISHING POLE
1 NOTEBOOK WITH DATA
2 BOXES STRAWBERRY POP-TARTS, FROSTED
4 CANS SWEET TEA
2 PACKS BUBBLEGUM CARDS
JOIE DE VIVRE
ELVIRA BROWN

THINGS I HAVE GAINED

POISON IVY
SUNBURN
DIARRHEA
22 SCABS
47 LUMPS AND BRUISES
108 SCRATCHES AND CUTS
5,000 CHIGGER BITES

THINGS I ONCE LOVED BUT NOW LOATHE

SUNRISE
SUNSET
SUNNY WEATHER
STORMY WEATHER
EVERYTHING GREEN
ANYTHING WET

Truman didn't have a bottle and it wouldn't matter if he did; he didn't have any paper or anything to write with. He considered how he might sign his farewell. "Having a Wonderful Time" would be the biggest of big fat lies.

As the night progressed, they poled alongside trees, stumps, and floating logs, pulling off Elvira's glowing galaxy of stars, comets, planets, and moons.

Before long, her trail led to a solid wall of moss-drenched cypresses, their roots buried in the water. Elvira's markers had led them to another narrow channel weaving between the trees.

Navigating through the tight spaces was hard work, but they struggled on. The moonlight was now all but blocked by dense branches and heavy moss. The air was thick and close.

It seemed there was nowhere left to go. They struggled into a nearly impenetrable stand of trees, and somehow pushed through. To their amazement, they found themselves entering a wide, moonlit lagoon. A fine mist rose from the surface. All around was silence. The lagoon was like an island of flat water, hidden in the heart of the swamp.

"Jeepers!" exclaimed Truman.

"Wow," said Nose. "I bet no one's been here in forever."

The lagoon did seem to have a magical quality, or perhaps it was just the relief of being out of the cloying dampness of the swamp and feeling the cool night air on their faces.

"This is just the kind of place where Ol' One Eye would live," said Sawyer.

"What if we run into him? Then what are we going to do?" asked Truman.

"Whatcha think we're gonna do?" said Nose. "We're gonna catch him."

"Catch him?" said Truman. "You roll all of us into one Incredible Hulk, we still couldn't catch him."

"What do you know about fishing, Einstein?"

"Not much. But I know something about the laws of physics."

"Them big city laws don't hold any sway out here," said Nose. "We got our own ways."

"Listen, say we did catch him. How would we get him out of the water?" Truman asked. "We'd need a lever. And a pulley. A tractor trailer would help, too."

"Look, guys," said Sawyer, "we find my sister first. Then we worry about Ol' One Eye."

After stopping to bail, they took up their poles again and soldiered on.

"What's that?" said Sawyer, pointing into the mist. A vague object was taking shape in the middle of the lagoon. As they poled in closer, they saw an aluminum rowboat—it was Moses's.

"Elvira—?" said Sawyer, his voice a mix of hope and fear.

They poled alongside and sat staring at the boat. It was empty, except for a few remaining pieces of gear.

"She's found dry land," Truman suggested.

"Yeah," agreed Nose. "Of course! She just forgot to tie up the boat."

The boys looked down at their feet. The water level in the pirogue continued to rise. There was nothing to do but abandon it and commandeer their old boat. They quickly set out again and began to holler into the mist.

"Virus! Virus!" shouted Nose.

"Don't call her that! Her name's Elvira!" said Sawyer.

"But—we always call her that."

"She doesn't like it. Okay?"

Nose shrugged as he and Truman exchanged glances. They joined Sawyer, their shouts filling the lagoon with cries of "Elvira."

17

LOST LAGOON

DAWN CREPT OVER THE LAGOON, TURNING THE CASTAWAYS' wake to a pale rose gold. The last of the storm clouds had cleared, and only a few dim stars lingered overhead. All around, the still, sleepy swamp began to stir. A morning mist thickened over the water, muffling their calls for Elvira.

On and on they poled, wondering just how wide the lagoon could possibly be. At last, the shadowy shapes of cypress crowns could be seen rising out of the mist.

Then—*what was that?* Sawyer thought they had gone in circles and wound up back at the flooded mansion. Some kind of ramshackle structure was looming in the fog—

They poled closer.

"A ship!" cried Sawyer.

"A g-ghost ship," said Truman.

"She's a paddlewheeler!" exclaimed Nose.

"A sternwheeler," Sawyer added, gazing up at the enormous wheel box. They were coming alongside the stern on the starboard side. The main deck was flooded aft, but rose from the lagoon amidships. She was listing slightly toward them, so that her port side was higher above the water.

By the look of her, she'd been stuck up here for ages. The swamp had grown in close, encroaching into the ship herself. Several cypress trees had erupted right through the weathered hull, their upper branches festooned with planking that had torn free and been carried aloft, a hundred feet overhead. A few years more and the swamp would swallow her completely.

Spanish moss draped from three dilapidated decks. A smokestack had toppled back into the trees. A tattered Confederate flag dangled from the jack staff. Faded lettering spelled out her name on the massive wheelbox.

"The *Delta Belle*," read Sawyer.

"A ghost ship!" repeated Truman.

"C'mon, Tru. A man of science like yourself oughta know there ain't no such thing as ghosts," said Nose.

"Ghosts—witches—gator eyes that aren't gator eyes—fish as big as whales—all of them wanting a piece of me." Truman shuddered. "I don't know what I believe anymore."

"Take it easy," said Sawyer. "It's just an old wreck."

"What's it doing out here in the middle of nowhere?" asked Truman.

"They prob'ly tried to hide her up here during the Civil

War," said Nose. "We learned about that in school, Saw, remember? They used to hide the riverboats up in the bayous so the Yankees couldn't find 'em. But so many people got killed in the war, some of the boats were forgotten and lost. Our teacher said there's still plenty of wrecks 'round these parts."

"Rivers do keep changing their course," said Truman. "I guess about a hundred years ago this used to be part of the Yazoo."

The boys rowed in closer. "Elvira!" they shouted. "Elviiiirah!"

"Sawyer! It's me! I'm here!"

They craned their necks and, sure enough, there she was on the main deck.

"Elvira!" called Sawyer.

"Sawyer!" she cried.

As the boys pushed forward, they saw a ragged black hole in the side of the ship, most of it below the waterline. "Looks like one of her boilers blew," said Sawyer. They oared past toward Elvira, who was jumping up and down, arms waving.

They came alongside where the main deck railing rose above the water. From there, they could climb aboard. Nose and Truman secured a mooring line as Elvira threw herself at Sawyer.

Sawyer scooped her up and swung her around and around. "You had us scared half to death!"

"I knew you'd find me!" she squealed.

"Why didn't you jump while you had a chance?"

"And let Ol' One Eye get away? I just couldn't!"

"Geez, Vi, you could've been killed!" said Sawyer, exasperated but relieved.

"You're pretty brave," said Truman.

Elvira beamed.

"Glad you're okay," said Nose awkwardly.

"Thanks!" she said.

The boys looked around. A once-grand staircase—now a wreck of peeling paint, misshapen molding, and broken rails—rose to the middle deck, which was circled by an ample promenade. A smaller staircase led from the promenade to the top deck. The broken windows of passenger cabins lined both upper decks. Above the uppermost deck was the pilothouse, its three rusty steam whistles still jutting from the roof.

Next to the main staircase, some of their gear lay in a jumbled heap.

"Hey," said Truman, "my snorkel stuff!"

"Come on," said Elvira, pulling Sawyer's arm. "I gotta show you something—"

"Wait—" said Nose, who was sifting through the pile. "Where's the food, Viru—uh—Vi?" he said. "I'm starved."

Elvira shook her head. "No food," she said.

"No food?" said Nose.

"What happened to it?" asked Truman.

"Ol' One Eye," said Elvira.

"He towed you all the way here?" said Sawyer.

"He's here, alright," said Elvira. "I tried to unload the rowboat, but he came up under and knocked most everything out. I think he ate the tackle box."

"Where'd he go?" asked Truman.

"Dunno," said Elvira, pulling Sawyer up the deck. "But come on, come on, hurry."

"Hurry where?" asked Sawyer.

"It's a surprise. You'll see. This way!" She let go of his arm and scurried up the deck toward the bow. "Look," she said, pointing through an ornate double doorway. They peered inside.

Nose gave a low whistle.

They entered what must have been the main salon. Clearly, the ship had once been quite elegant. Directly in front of them, across the vast room, broken windows opened out into the dense swamp on the port side. The empty panes were still flanked by tattered red velvet drapes.

At the far end, an immense gilt-framed mirror, its surface tarnished and cracked, dominated the wall. In the middle of the warped plank floor stood a cast-iron stove with copper trim that had long since turned green. Three elaborate chandeliers hung precariously from a beamed ceiling. Threadbare sofas and rotting velvet armchairs were strewn every which way.

Elvira fidgeted impatiently. "Over there!" She pointed. "See?"

The boys gazed in openmouthed wonder at a battered riverman's trunk.

Or was it a pirate's chest?

"Eureka!" exclaimed Truman. "The treasure!"

"Treasure?" asked Elvira.

"She found it," said Nose.

"But it's—" began Elvira.

The boys charged across the room. Nose was first to the trunk. Sawyer and Truman crowded around. Nose lifted the lid. Their expectant looks vanished.

Nestled in a mound of moldy clothes was an odd-looking bird.

"What is that?" said Truman.

"He's a wood stork, silly," said Elvira. "He's just a little baby."

"Wow, first time I've ever seen a real one," said Truman.

"It's just a stupid stork," said Nose. He rummaged through the clothing. "Maybe the treasure's buried under here somewhere."

Sawyer shook his head. "Yeah, right. Maybe it laid some golden eggs. When we're through here, we'll go lookin' for the golden harp," he snickered.

Nose's eyes widened. He held up some rusty coins. "Hey, Sawyer. Doubloons! We're rich!"

Truman took a coin from Nose and inspected it, rubbing at the rust and dirt. "Sorry, Nose," he said. "But these are casino chips." He handed one to Sawyer.

"*Delta Belle*," read Sawyer. "You can still see the imprint."

Nose rolled his eyes, then said, "Hey, maybe there's a

craps table in here somewhere," shaking the coins in his palm. He let them fly with an underhand toss, like he'd seen his uncles do when they played dice games. The coins scattered in all directions across the warped floor, and some fell through the cracks into the water below.

Down in the murky water, the coins glinted in the pearly light. A ponderous white shape glided through the submerged hull. A gaping mouth stretched open. The coins vanished.

"Nice treasure, Vi," teased Nose.

She lifted the baby stork and cradled it. "He's so cute, isn't he? He must've fallen out of his nest. Can I keep him, Sawyer, can I?"

Sawyer sighed. "I think you need a nap, Vi."

"Why? I'm not sleepy."

"'Cause *we* need the rest—"

A shudder rippled through the floorboards.

"What was that?" whispered Elvira.

Another shudder seemed to come from below. They looked down at their feet.

"Something's coming," said Sawyer.

Then the floor seemed to settle. They all held their breath. They looked at each other. They looked at their feet. They listened—

Just when they were about to heave a sigh of relief—

BAM! Something huge rammed into the floor from below. Ten square feet of the century-old planks began to buckle.

"Ol' One Eye!" shouted Nose.

"He's back!" screeched Elvira.

"Yikes!" said Sawyer.

The room shuddered again as the floor took another hit. Vermin of all kinds showered from the rafters. Roaches, crickets, ants, termites—the floor was writhing with creepy-crawlies.

Elvira shrieked even louder, trying to shield the bird and her hair at once.

"He's coming up!" hollered Truman.

WHAM! The beast must have thrown all his weight behind one great lunge. Floorboards began to splinter with an awful rending sound. A hole opened in the floor, with jagged cracks spreading in all directions.

Water surged through and washed across the planks. Everyone stared at the opening.

WHOOSH! Ol' One Eye's whiskered mouth filled the hole and thrashed from side to side.

"Let's go! Go! GO!" yelled Sawyer, grabbing Elvira's hand.

Sawyer, Elvira, and Nose bolted for the door, vaulting over cracks zigzagging in their path. Vermin swarmed crazily.

Truman skidded to a stop as a chasm opened before him, blocking his escape and separating him from the others.

"Guys—?" he called out. But it was too late. They had vanished through the doorway.

Sawyer, Elvira, and Nose charged down the deck back to their rowboat. It was drifting on its mooring line about ten feet from the ship. Sawyer grabbed the rope and began to haul. Nose reached for the bow.

The rowboat flipped topsy-turvy into the air, snapping the line. What little remained in the bottom of the boat was scattered across the water. Ol' One Eye reared his head, and the boat came down hard with a heavy splash. They stepped back quickly.

"There goes our ride," said Sawyer.

The amazing creature swam in lazy circles, sucking down their things with voracious glee.

Elvira looked around. "Where's Tru?"

18

DELTA BELLE

TRUMAN WAS TRAPPED ON AN ISLAND OF PLANKING. There was nowhere to go but into the water. The accordion still strapped to his back, he took a deep breath, held his nose, and jumped.

Sawyer, Nose, and Elvira ran back to the doorway and peered into the salon, but Truman was nowhere in sight. They called out, but there was no answer.

"I told him to get rid of that squawk box," said Nose. "He couldn't outrun a mud turtle with that thing around his neck. But no. He wouldn't—"

"We can't be sure," said Sawyer. "He may be, well, he, maybe he's . . ." He stopped and they looked at each other, a grim realization dawning.

They walked back down the deck toward their rowboat.

Ol' One Eye had nosed it some distance into the lagoon. Sawyer scooped up the broken mooring line and sighed.

"Poor old Tru," said Nose, nudging Truman's snorkel with his toe.

"What do we do now?" Elvira moaned.

The rowboat was out of reach. It might as well have been in the next county. Ol' One Eye could show up again at any minute. And Truman was lost.

Sawyer looked around at the ship.

"Head for higher ground," he decided, pointing to the pilothouse.

Below decks, Truman found a pocket of air on the port side, which sat a little higher above the water. Taking another deep breath, he dove, seeking a way out. Nothing. He came up for air and dove again. It was too dark to see anything in the black water. He surfaced, gulped some air, and dove again. This time, he could make out a doorway beside a submerged staircase.

He swam closer. Was that—light? Yes, he could definitely see a dim patch of light through the open doorway at the end of the murky hall. He came up for air and then, diving and kicking with all his might, he made for the light.

Sawyer mounted the main staircase. "I'll go first," he said, testing his weight on the lowest step.

"Hold on," said Elvira. She turned to their remaining

gear, which was still piled next to the landing. "I have to make a nest for my stork."

She found a jacket and laid it out. "You two better stay here," she whispered as she settled the bird and Barbie together.

Sawyer and Nose rolled their eyes.

Carefully they made their way up the rickety decks, around rotting holes and over buckled wood. Higher and higher they climbed. On the upper deck they found a stairway ascending to the pilothouse atop the ship.

At the head of the stairs, the pilothouse door hung half off its hinges. It creaked as they pushed their way inside. The room was in shambles, except for the ship's steering wheel.

Elvira grabbed one of the spokes radiating from the hub. The wheel was nearly twice as tall as she was.

"Wow," breathed Nose. "Look at the size of it."

"Look how high we are," said Sawyer. "I bet on a clear day you could see for miles from up here."

Sawyer thought he could make out a channel running off into the mist. "Hey." He pointed. "That could be the way out of here."

Nose squinted. "Looks like it's goin' in the right direction. Maybe it runs into the Yazoo."

Off the bow they could see the gangplank, hanging from a derrick by a giant hook. Sawyer was already familiar with the apparatus from his model boats. When the ship was underway, the gangplank projected in front. At anchor, it could be swung over either side and lowered ashore. This design allowed steamboats to dock easily on both sides of a river. Sawyer could see the winch on the forward deck, which had been used for the raising and lowering.

"That sure is one big hook," he murmured.

Elvira interrupted his thoughts. "How much longer you think he's gonna keep doing that?" she asked, scowling at Ol' One Eye, who had returned to toss around their rowboat with his beer-barrel snout.

"Till he decides to start tossing us around," replied Nose.

As if he'd overheard, Ol' One Eye dove and vanished. He soon reappeared, gave a mighty heave, and tossed the craft thirty feet in the air, like a toy. The rowboat splashed down noisily, landing upside down.

"He sure likes to rub it in," Nose said.

Truman pushed through the muddy water toward the light. His lungs burning, he pulled himself through the doorway at the end of the hall and pushed for the surface. He gasped for air. As the oxygen flowed back into his chest, he saw the paddlewheel looming above him. He had surfaced inside the wheel box.

The paneling which covered the wheel had rotted away in many places, and dawn light filtered through. Truman realized he had to get out of the water before Ol' One Eye came back. There must have been a ladder here, in bygone days, to climb down to the wheel for repairs. If he found it, he could climb up and squeeze through to the deck.

He splashed around. There was no trace of a ladder on the port side. He swam across to starboard, marveling at the size of the paddlewheel. It must have been twenty-five feet in diameter. On the opposite side, he found what he expected, but it was no help. A wooden ladder had once been bolted to the interior hull, but the rungs had long since rotted away. The walls themselves were slick with algae.

He dog-paddled over to the great wheel and grasped the lowest slat. The wood here was also rotting, but he'd have to climb it.

Truman held on for a moment, catching his breath. He thought he heard a splash. Was Ol' One Eye coming for him? He listened, but there was nothing more.

Climb, Truman, climb, he told himself, but his body didn't respond. He'd hardly slept or eaten since yesterday morning. He rested his head against his arm.

In a minute, he thought, *just give yourself a minute.*

Finally, he began to climb, slat by slat along the curve of the wheel. He was making good progress when he spotted a pale, blunt shape rising from the depths. In an instant, Ol' One Eye's head broke the surface and slammed down on the paddle slat nearest the water, shattering it.

The impact almost knocked Truman off the wheel. The paddle descended with a groan, lowering him several feet closer to the water.

Truman started to climb again, but something was wrong. He was stuck!

Stay calm, stay calm, he told himself, *don't panic.*

It took all his will not to scream. Keeping his eyes on the massive fish, he felt around to see where he was caught. It was the accordion strap! It had become tangled around one of the paddles.

Quickly, quietly, he worked to shed the strap. His hands shook. It was almost loose when—

Ol' One Eye reared his monstrous snout and again slammed down on the nearest slat, smashing it to bits. The paddlewheel shuddered. Again it groaned and rotated downward. Truman clung on.

The wheel continued to descend, bringing him closer and closer to Ol' One Eye's blubbery breadbasket. As Truman struggled to reach the slat above, his accordion strap snapped, and the bulky instrument bounced down the wheel toward that cavernous albino mouth.

High above, in the pilothouse, Sawyer, Nose, and Elvira looked out over the lagoon.

"Do you really think Ol' One Eye might have Mom's ring?" asked Elvira. Sawyer had just told her the real reason behind their quest.

"I don't know," he said, "but Moses says that even miracles can happen in Catfish Time."

"Truman's gonna need a miracle, too," said Nose.

"Unless he's already with the angels, playing his accordian right now, in heaven. With all those harps," said Elvira.

Sawyer heard a sound. "Shhh. Listen—"

Nose and Elvira heard it, too. There was no mistaking

the distant moan of an accordion. They looked around.

"Tru—?"

"Truman—?"

"Truman!"

They tumbled out of the pilothouse toward the sound. They paused on the promenade deck, leaned over the rail, and listened.

There it was again, a far-off wail. It seemed to come from an open hatch on the bow of the main deck. They made their way down the rickety stairs, then ran up the deck to the hatch.

There they could see an iron railing that had once served as a ladder, descending into what looked like a corridor below. They climbed down and found themselves below decks in a cramped, low-ceilinged passage that had evidently been used for storage.

Wooden crates and a rusty chain were piled to one side of the ladder. Several buoys were heaped against the bulkhead. Another short passage led to a door.

"Engine room?" asked Nose.

They heard a muffled accordion moan coming from behind the door.

"He's in there!" said Sawyer.

Sawyer crept down the passage and opened the door. Nose and Elvira crowded behind him.

"Truman?" called Elvira.

They peered into the darkness of the flooded engine room. Ancient machinery lay strewn all around. At the far end, the chamber was fully submerged. At their end, water lapped up along the floor just a few feet from the doorway. On the starboard side they could see sunlight shafting through the dark hole from the boiler explosion.

But there was no evidence of Truman.

"Truman! Truman!" they called. Nothing.

They turned back toward the ladder as the door creaked shut behind them. They heard it again! It *was* the accordion, coming from behind that door.

"Truman—?" said Sawyer, moving back toward the engine room.

"Ah, guys—"

They spun around. Truman clung to the top of the ladder behind them, soaking wet. "I don't think you want to open that," he said.

But the steamboat suddenly heaved and lurched, and the door flew open as water surged into the passage, sweeping the others off their feet. They scrambled for the ladder, slipping and sliding on the sloping floor. Elvira got there first. Truman grabbed her hand and pushed her up ahead of him. Nose clambered close behind.

Sawyer belly flopped for the bottom rung as Nose stretched for his hand. Another wave surged in and washed Sawyer aside. He slid back down to the doorway and almost poured through. Just in time, his jeans snagged on the door jam, stopping him mere inches from sliding into the engine room.

"Sawyer, look out!" shouted Elvira.

That monstrous missile-headed cat was emerging from the water and easing itself UP THE FLOOR!—its hideous mouth opening and closing. An accordion moan seemed to be coming from deep inside Ol' One Eye's belly.

"Holy cow!" exclaimed Nose. "He swallowed Einstein's squawk box!"

"Haaaaallp!" Sawyer yowled.

A yard of fish face floundered toward him, with wriggling, arm's-length whiskers and stubby teeth gleaming between pendulous lips. In place of one eye was a ghastly, scarred socket.

Nose, Truman, and Elvira watched horror-struck as Ol' One Eye hauled himself farther toward the door, his slobbery lips wrapping around Sawyer's left ankle. Sawyer kicked like crazy and clawed at the slimy floor, but he couldn't gain any traction.

"Do something!" hollered Sawyer. "He's gonna eat meeee!!!"

Nose looked around. The chain! It was piled in the corner. He grabbed one end and tossed it toward Sawyer.

"Saw!" he called. "Reach!"

Sawyer strained, but the chain fell short.

"Human chain!" Nose yelled. "C'mon, guys!"

Nose climbed down the ladder and gripped the bottom rung with one hand. Truman followed, gripping Nose's other hand, and then Elvira. They formed a brigade, and Elvira tossed the chain.

Sawyer grabbed hold. Nose, Truman, and Elvira pulled one way and the behemoth cat pulled the other, in a desperate tug-of-war with Sawyer stretched in the middle.

"Sawyer!" screamed Elvira.

"Kick him, kick him!" yelled Truman.

"Hang on, we gotcha!" shouted Nose.

Sawyer kicked wildly at the fish's one good eye, and inch by inch his foot slipped from the drooling maw. The others dragged him to the ladder. Screaming, they heaved themselves up.

Like a vision in a cold nightmare, the leviathan lunged after them. The door frame shattered as Ol' One Eye burst through. He lumbered up the passage, using his spiny fins like arms. The floor trembled and groaned beneath his weight, the accordion moan still coming from his open mouth.

Truman, Nose, Elvira, and Sawyer scrambled out through the hatch, hollering and giddy with near hysteria. One by one, they sank to the deck in a heap.

"Am I loony?" Truman wheezed. "Or was that fish *walking* up the hall?"

"You're loony all right," panted Nose, "and he *was* walking up the hall!"

"Saw a picture once of a catfish taking a stroll across a Florida highway," said Sawyer, shaking his head. "Never really believed it till now." He rubbed his ankle.

"You okay?" asked Nose.

"Think so." Sawyer pulled up his pant leg. "He mostly got my sneaker."

Sawyer rolled down his sock to reveal several nasty-looking scratches.

"Lemme see that," said Nose, bending to examine Sawyer's wounds.

"Elvira, over here!" called Truman. He was dragging debris and piling it over the trapdoor. She ran to help while Nose ripped up his T-shirt and used it to bandage Sawyer's ankle.

"You know, Saw—" said Nose, lowering his voice. "I guess—well—I was wrong about Ol' Two Eye."

"That's okay," said Sawyer. "Who could've believed how big Ol' One Eye really is?"

Truman glanced over at Sawyer and Nose. "Is he—bleeding?"

"Relax, Einstein. We won't need to amputate," said Nose. Truman turned away.

"You look like you're going to throw up," said Elvira.

"Aren't your parents supposed to be doctors or something?" asked Nose.

"My dad's a pharmacist and my mom's a nurse. I guess I didn't inherit a stomach for medicine." Truman shrugged.

"Good as new," pronounced Nose as he finished with the makeshift bandage.

The hatch was battened, and Sawyer was safe.

"Now what?" said Elvira.

"Guess we know what it means to be up a creek without a paddle," said Nose.

"Paddle?" said Sawyer. "We don't even have a boat!"

19

EGG EYE

THEY SAT ON THE DECK OF THE *DELTA BELLE*, WONDERING what would come next. The last of the stars had winked out, and the early birds were starting to sing.

Elvira had retrieved her stork and her Barbie and sat with them cradled in her arms.

"There ain't no fish like Ol' One Eye in the history of time!" said Nose.

"And he's testing us," said Truman. "He wants to see how good we are."

"He wants to see how good we taste." Sawyer laughed.

"Speaking of taste—I'm starved," said Elvira.

The boys stared pointedly at her stork. Elvira scooted back, hugging the baby bird.

"There sure are a lot of birds 'round here," mused Nose,

eyeing a heron gliding overhead. "Wish I had my slingshot. I'd get us some breakfast."

Sawyer followed his gaze. He scrambled to his feet.

"Hey, look at that!" Sawyer gestured toward a nest high in a treetop.

"What about it?" said Truman absently.

"I'm going up!"

"What in the world for?" asked Truman. "You planning to snare a heron?"

The sun crested the horizon behind the trees. Nose, Truman, and Elvira stood on top of the pilothouse, looking up into the branches. Sawyer was climbing a tall cypress that towered through the deck. He lugged a bucket containing a long length of rope and gradually made his way closer to the nest.

As he hauled himself into the upper limbs, he saw that the nest was even larger than he had guessed. It must have been more than three feet wide. A pair of nesting storks took flight, startling Sawyer.

The others gasped as Sawyer slipped. They held their breath until he regained his footing.

"That was close!" breathed Nose.

Sawyer peeked over the rim of the nest. A clutch of stork eggs was tucked inside—five of them, each bigger than a tennis ball. He made a bed of cypress needles in the bottom of the bucket and gently loaded the eggs. Tying one end of the rope around the handle, he lowered the pail to his waiting companions.

As Sawyer began his descent, the others gathered around the pail, looking hungrily at the eggs.

"Good job, Saw!" said Nose, as Sawyer reached the top of the pilothouse.

"Right on!" said Truman.

Half an hour later, they had set up a camp on deck at the bottom of the main staircase. Nose was boiling four of the eggs over a small fire. They had decided to save the last egg for a meager lunch.

They had found the ship's galley just off the dining room on the promenade deck. There they'd scrounged a soup pot to use as a fire pit and a smaller pot to cook the eggs.

Sawyer kept watch for any sign of Ol' One Eye while Nose crouched by the fire, tending the eggs.

"Time for breakfast!" Nose called. He lifted the pot off the fire and dished out four enormous soft-boiled eggs.

Elvira eyeballed her egg. She was terribly hungry, but the baby stork was gazing at her. She stopped in mid-bite.

"Don't worry." She sighed. "I won't eat it. I promise."

Truman peeled his egg. "I'm eating mine!" he said, biting into it. Yellow yolk squirted down his chin.

"This is no three-minute egg," he complained. "I specifically ordered a three-minute egg."

"Hey, Einstein, why don't you take your egg and shove it in your ear for another minute or two. Then, when you cool off, it should be right at three minutes."

"My mother says it has to be exactly three minutes. Any more or less could lead to excessive bowel movements," said Truman.

"Well, maybe when we get back, your mommy can make you a perfect egg," replied Nose.

"Hey, at least I have a mother," Truman blurted.

Sawyer and Elvira stared at him.

"We still have our mom, don't we, Sawyer?"

"Just eat your egg."

Elvira looked at her egg. She looked at the baby stork. Maybe she wasn't so hungry after all. Idly she played with the egg. She rummaged in her Barbie lunch box, found a tiny eye pencil in Barbie's makeup case, and began to draw on the egg. Lashes, pupil, iris—she turned it into a big staring eye.

Truman looked at Sawyer. "Aw, man. I'm sorry."

"Hey, Saw never wanted you along in the first place," said Nose. "All your whining and fancy words. And that crappy hog callin' you call music."

Elvira tried to distract them. "Hey, look at me. I'm Ol' One Eye."

She held the decorated egg to her eye, squinting her other eye and puckering her lips.

"Fish face!" She giggled. "Betcha can't catch me!" Elvira playfully dashed around. The boys, who were nowhere near a playful mood, watched sullenly.

"Get back here, Elvira!" snapped Sawyer.

"Betcha can't catch Ol' One Eye!" she teased.

Elvira tripped. Her foot struck her Barbie lunch box and sent it skidding toward a ragged hole in the deck. "Oh no!" she cried, as the lunch box—with Barbie inside—went tumbling down the hole.

The lunch box fell open, spilling Barbie and all her gear into the black water.

"Barbie!" Elvira called. She got down on her knees and reached, but it was too far.

Just then, Ol' One Eye's humongous head lurched from the water, mouth stretched wider than wide, engulfing Barbie, the lunch box, and all its contents.

Startled, Elvira lost her balance. "Aaaahhh!" she screamed, as she tumbled in.

Sawyer, Nose, and Truman dashed across the deck. They could see Elvira standing in chest-high water ten feet below in the flooded hull. She seemed paralyzed, still clutching her egg.

"Elvira, you okay?" shouted Sawyer.

"He ate my Barbie! He's gonna eat me!"

Reflected water danced off the ceiling. In the dim light, she made out Ol' One Eye's white shape plowing a huge circle. He turned and began to swim her way.

"Haaaaallp! He's comiiiinnng!" she squealed. Ol' One Eye bore down on her.

"Get away from me!" she shouted, throwing her egg at him.

Just inches away, the fish veered off and made a beeline for the egg.

"I'll throw down a rope! We'll bring you up!" called Sawyer.

"No! He'll get me! I know he will!"

"Where is he? Can you see him?" asked Nose.

"Yes!"

"What's he doing?" asked Sawyer.

"Playing with his food!"

"He's what?" said Sawyer.

"Playing with my egg! Do something!"

Ol' One Eye was some distance off, spewing out a jet of water. He launched the egg high in the air and swam after it. He scooped it back in his mouth, and spewed it out again.

"He went after the egg? That makes no sense," said Nose.

Sawyer tried to puzzle it out. "Wait—a—minute," he said. "Makes perfect sense. We got one left. Go get it!"

"Get—what?" said Truman.

"The egg, the last egg!" shouted Sawyer.

"What are we gonna do? Egg him?" asked Nose.

"What's the one thing Ol' One Eye doesn't have?" said Sawyer. "The one thing he needs to be like every other fish in the Yazoo?"

"An eye! He wants his eye back!" cried Truman.

"A-plus, Einstein. That's why he went after the egg instead of Vi," Nose said. "An egg instead of an eye—like one of your meta—meta-lures."

"A metaphor! Yeah!" said Truman. "We're going to

use a real live metaphor to catch Ol' One Eye, aren't we, Sawyer?"

"We're gonna try. Go get me that egg."

Truman dashed back to fetch the last egg.

Sawyer knelt over the hole. He gestured to the rafters crisscrossing the upper section of the hull.

"Climb up there," he called to Elvira. "You'll be safe. I'll get you out."

"I'm scared, Sawyer," said Elvira.

"Just do it. I'm gonna come get you," Sawyer reassured her.

They watched as she climbed into the upper portion of the hull.

"Attagirl," said Sawyer. "Truman—gimme that egg. Quick."

Truman snatched up the egg, turned, stumbled, and fell. The egg seemed to hang in the air for a horrible instant and then dropped to the deck.

SPLAT.

20

CAT BAIT

EVERYONE STARED AT THE SPLATTERED EGG. "SMOOTH move!" said Nose. "Now what?"

"Sawyer! Hurry!" cried Elvira.

"Hold on! I'm coming!" Sawyer shouted. "We gotta find something to lure Ol' One Eye away from Elvira. In case he comes back."

Sawyer turned to Nose and Truman.

"C'mon, guys," said Sawyer. "Think fast."

"What goes good with eggs?" asked Nose.

"I like mine with Spam," said Sawyer.

"Then we're outta luck. They didn't have cans way back then," said Nose.

"Sure they did," said Truman. "Thermal processing was invented in 1809 in France as a way of preserving food for military use."

Sawyer and Nose blinked.

"The galley!" said Truman.

The boys bolted for the stairs, running as fast as they could on the rotting wood.

"HANG ON, VI—" called Sawyer over his shoulder.

"*Saw—yer,*" came her small voice from the hole. "*Hur—ry!*"

They rushed to the galley and began searching through the cupboards. Plates, bowls, silverware, teacups, and saucers. But no canned goods.

Nose opened what looked like a closet. "Mother lode!" he yelped. "The pantry!"

An avalanche of canned goods began to form on the floor as the boys ransacked the dusty pantry. They filled their arms and rushed back to the deck.

Sawyer grabbed a gallon can of Old Dominion oysters. The antique tin had a lid like a paint can. "Jackknife," he called.

Nose flipped open his knife and helped with the lid. They heard a hiss as the century-old air escaped. Sawyer and Truman fell back, choking from the stench.

Nose took a deep whiff. "Are you sure Ol' One Eye's gonna smell this?" he asked.

"Are you kidding?" said Truman. "He'll smell this a mile off."

Sawyer stripped down to his swimming trunks and began smearing the fetid goo all over his body. "Step on it, guys," he urged. Truman and Nose pitched in, prying open cans and turning Sawyer into a human bait ball.

They'd found Punch & Judy biscuits, Ghirardelli cocoa, Dixie Dawn-brand ground coffee, and Happenbach's summer sausage. There was even a package of Mason's boot blacking and a can of Union Leader tobacco.

Soon the deck was littered with empty, stinking cans. "Sure you know what you're doing?" asked Nose.

Sawyer, caked from head to foot with the putrid mess, turned to Nose. "DO I LOOK LIKE I KNOW WHAT I'M DOING?" he squawked.

He ran down the deck and grabbed Truman's snorkel gear. He pulled on the mask, plugged the snorkel in his mouth, and slipped on the flippers.

"Get the rope," he called to Nose. Then, trailing the foul aroma, he slipped through the hole and disappeared into the hull.

Elvira looked down from the rafters at Sawyer, wading toward her. Then the smell hit her. "UGH! Sawyer! What are you doing!"

"Climb down," said Sawyer. "I'll tie this around you." He took hold of the rope that Nose and Truman were lowering. "They'll pull you up. Hurry."

Elvira climbed down to Sawyer. He began wrapping the rope under her arms. Suddenly, she screamed.

"Sawyer!"

Behind him, a gargantuan white shape emerged from the water. It swam rapidly toward them.

Sawyer quickly secured the rope around his sister. "Pull!" he yelled.

Ol' One Eye was just a yard off when Sawyer dove out of harm's way. Nose and Truman pulled on the rope, swinging Elvira up and over the charging fish.

She swung toward Ol' One Eye. But the fish dove back into the depths, after a stinky lure—Sawyer Brown.

In the murky water, Sawyer swam for his life—past tree trunks, around a jumble of rotting beams and collapsed decking, among a tumble of ancient machinery.

He surfaced to take in air and get his bearings. To his surprise, he banged his head. He was somewhere in the submerged hull, and there was now just six inches between his chin and the ceiling. But there was no sign of the monster fish.

Sawyer dipped under again, turned in a complete circle—and found himself face-to-face with Ol' One Eye!

Sawyer bolted, swimming without any sense of direction. Ol' One Eye head-butted and thrashed between beams and planks, shifting them like matchsticks, hunting for the stinky bait.

Sawyer struggled to find his way through the jumbled labyrinth. He spotted daylight and swam for it, Ol' One Eye close on his heels. A black hole framed by twisted metal came into focus. It was the exploded boiler. The steam pipe made a passageway through the underwater maze and was open on the opposite end.

Sawyer entered the long tube, kicking hard. The

behemoth cat followed, swinging his tail. The prodigious appendage swished through the water as Ol' One Eye pushed himself into the pipe after Sawyer. The surging water shifted the litter of beams. They collapsed, sealing off the sunken entrance.

Sawyer emerged through the open boiler door at the other end. He turned. Ol' One Eye's broad mouth was coming at him, and fast. With his last bit of strength, Sawyer swung the door shut, dropped the latch, and punched through to the surface, gasping for air.

The boiler shuddered. Ol' One Eye was trapped!

Nose, Truman, and Elvira peered down the hole where Sawyer had disappeared. Air bubbles rose. One flipper bobbed into view: a chunk was missing.

"Sawyer?" murmured Nose.

Sawyer abruptly surfaced, scarfing down air. Nose and Truman hauled him up with the rope. "I got him!—I trapped him in one of the boilers!" Sawyer choked out.

"Trapped? Really?" said Nose.

"You got him, you got him!" squealed Elvira.

"Great!" said Truman, brushing off his hands. "We got Vi out. You're back. Everyone's safe. And Ol' One Eye's trapped. So, what do you say? Let's go home!"

Sawyer shook his head. "Not till I find what I came for."

"Come on, Sawyer," whined Truman. "There's no treasure."

"I seem to remember someone saying there wasn't any giant cat, either," said Sawyer. He turned to Nose. "Listen, he's trapped. But that boiler's not gonna hold him for long. If we're gonna go looking for his nest, we gotta make sure he's dead."

"We gotta bring him in," agreed Nose. "We'll never make the papers with just another fish story."

"But how?" said Truman. "We'd need a whale boat to reel in that monster."

Sawyer eyed the rust-caked winch and giant hook that had once been used to swing the gangplank. The others followed his gaze.

"Oh, no—" said Truman. "Is he thinking what I think he's thinking?"

"Sawyer's right," said Elvira. "If he gets loose and comes after us again, we might never get home."

The thought of Ol' One Eye chasing them all the way back to Belzoni put even Truman at a loss for words.

"Come on, guys," urged Sawyer. "We can do it. We can land that fish."

A glimmer of hope lit their tired eyes.

"Well, if you're the man with the plan," said Nose, "then I guess we can lend a hand!"

21

CAT FIGHT

THE MORNING WAS GRAY AND MUGGY. MIST SHROUDED the lagoon. All hands on deck, Sawyer, Nose, Elvira, and Truman made ready for their confrontation with the great albino beast.

They first had to prepare the winch, but it was stuck fast. Try as they might, they couldn't make it budge.

They found some rusty tools in a rusty metal box and set to work, banging and clanging and chipping away until their hands and faces were a reddish brown, as if they, too, had turned to rust.

Finally, they were able to swing the derrick around toward the hole in the deck. Nose, Truman, and Elvira manned the crank, lowering the iron hook on its frayed steel cable and letting out plenty of slack.

Sawyer looped the cable around his thin chest and under

his arms. He hefted the heavy hook through the cable and cinched it tight. Then he slipped on Truman's goggles. After a last adjustment, he turned to the winch crew and gave a firm nod.

His mates joined hands cranking the stiff cable, lifting him gradually off the sloping deck. They swung the derrick so that Sawyer was dangling directly over the yawning hole. Then they reversed the winch and gradually let out the cable. Sawyer began his descent.

Elvira left the winch and went to the hole. Down Sawyer went, closer and closer to the water. He breathed deep, preparing to go under. His feet touched the water. Elvira signaled the winchers to hold.

"You sure about this, Sawyer?" she asked.

"Lower away!" he yelled.

Inch by inch, the warm, turbid water crept up his legs, his waist, his chest, his chin. Sawyer took a final breath and nodded. Elvira nodded to Nose and Truman. The water covered Sawyer's mouth, his nose, his eyes—and he was gone.

Six feet beneath the surface, Sawyer's groping toes settled atop the boiler. Straddling it, he unhooked the cable. He stretched out atop the cylinder, grasping the hook in one hand.

When the cable went slack, Nose and Truman released the winch. The cable could now run free.

Leaning over the boiler door, Sawyer tried to raise

the latch. It was stuck. He strained and tried again. It refused to budge. With a third effort, the door swung open.

Expecting the worst, Sawyer scooted back and braced himself, but nothing happened. He waited, but still nothing. He inched forward, bent close, and stared into the boiler mouth. It was pitch black inside.

Without warning, Ol' One Eye's pale face lunged from the dark and exploded through the open hatch. The hinged door tumbled aside. It happened so fast that Sawyer had no time to cram the hook in the creature's mouth. Instead, he threw himself around Ol' One Eye's neck and held on tight as foot after foot of catfish wriggled from the black hole. The colossal cat carried him off through the pearly green water.

Nose, Truman, and Elvira felt a sudden tension in the cable and immediately began to winch. But it was no use. Ol' One Eye at top speed was too strong. The cable tightened and was dragged down the hole, yard by yard, scraping all the way.

Sawyer's lungs screamed for air. The undulating cat descended, then cruised along the muddy bottom, plowing through a vast bed of eel grass. Long strands whipped past. A school of nervous needle-nosed gar darted to their right. To their left, an astonished mud turtle barely avoided an aquatic shell bender.

The cat spun clockwise trying to dislodge Sawyer, who might've lost his grip if it hadn't been for the cable now binding him to a ton of spongy fish flesh. The cat began to ascend.

Elvira spotted something out in the lagoon. "Look! It's Sawyer!" she shouted.

There he was, Sawyer Brown, holding on for dear, sweet life, his goggles speckled with duckweed, gulping air before the cat could submerge again. The fish wove to and fro with wide sweeps of his scarred and tattered tail. It was hard to tell if Ol' One Eye was annoyed or merely enjoying himself. He dove under again.

The lagoon surged and settled. The team on the deck swallowed hard and strained to see, but there was sign of neither boy nor fish.

Then, wonder of wonders, Ol' One Eye leapt from the water once more, as if launched from a circus cannon. Out and out and up and up, and still there was more of him, until he hovered in the air, more bird than fish.

And Sawyer Brown rode him bareback. The supercat performed a slow somersault, dove, and parted a patch of water celery with a tremendous WALLOP!

"That cat's gotta be part salmon!" Nose marveled.

Ol' One Eye continued weaving as Sawyer tried to struggle free. The cat launched again from the water, this time higher than before, as if showing off. The mighty fish performed another flip and splashed down.

Nose, Truman, and Elvira watched anxiously from the deck of the *Delta Belle*.

Beneath the surface, Ol' One Eye now rolled counterclockwise. The cable unwrapped and Sawyer pushed away, still clutching the huge hook.

Ol' One Eye must have felt Sawyer break free because the monster now turned to face him. The great fish paused, and for a moment Sawyer thought he was about to swim off. Then, that whale of a catfish rushed forward in an all-out charge.

The gaping mouth was just a few yards away and closing fast. Sawyer thrust his arms out in self-defense and—CHOMP! WHOOSH!

To Sawyer's amazement, he was still free and in one piece—though he no longer held the hook. He kicked for the surface. Glancing back, he glimpsed Ol' One Eye, barreling away and trailing a frayed steel cable. The monster had chomped down on the shiny metal. Ol' One Eye was hooked!

Sawyer, Nose, and Elvira watched as the catfish broke the surface and sailed through the air.

"Where's Sawyer?" cried Elvira.

Ol' One Eye's previous leaps were only warm-ups. Up and up and up he went, into the pale sunlight, and there, in defiance of all known laws of gravity, he hung and shook himself. Cascading spray caught the light, casting a hundred rainbows. The sleek cat—with the steel cable dangling from his mouth—shivered and plunged back into the water.

"Jumpin' Jehosaphat!" exclaimed Nose.

"Magnificent," murmured Truman.

"The winch! To the winch!" hollered Elvira, springing forward. Nose and Truman rushed to their posts.

. . .

Sawyer emerged, gasping for breath, hidden among swamp grass and cattails. *Ol' One Eye's bound to be madder than the Devil on Sunday, with that hook in his mouth,* he thought. He made his way back to the *Delta Belle* and slid into a hollow just inside the hull.

Nose, Truman, and Elvira struggled to steady the winch as Ol' One Eye veered hard. The derrick shuddered and groaned. The cable bent at a sharp angle. Rusty rivets popped and ancient planks began to shred. That fighting fish was tearing the winch right off the ship!

"Hang on!" yelled Nose.

They were thrown off their feet as the deck broke apart, but they held on to the winch. A section sheared away—derrick, winch, fishermen, and all—and pancaked into the water. The titanic beast was towing them across the lagoon!

They scrambled to their feet.

"Keep cranking!" said Truman.

And they did just that. They cranked and cranked and cranked, fighting the Jurassic cat.

Sawyer peered out from his hiding place and pulled off his goggles. He was on the opposite side of the ship now, where the swamp came up close. He had to find his way back to the others, but he wasn't looking forward to another near-death experience with Ol' One Eye. As he glanced around, he caught sight of something bobbing in the water. Splashing over, he discovered the Barbie lunch box.

Nose, Truman, and Elvira stayed steady at the winch. Rolling waves slapped against the sides of the severed deck, but they kept to their work. They seemed to be making progress. It was three against one, and now Ol' One Eye was fighting for his life.

Sawyer swam along the port side of the *Delta Belle*. He figured to come around the stern and find a way back on deck. The sun was well up, and he could see below the surface. He kept a lookout for any sign of Ol' One Eye.

He discovered another large hole in the hull. Pulling on the goggles, he dove down to investigate.

The ragged hole led farther into the hull. He saw something glinting on the muddy bottom.

Kicking harder, he swam down to scoop up the shiny object. It was a rusty dog tag shaped like a bone. He slipped it into the lunch box. As Sawyer came up for air, he thought he spied another object sparkling from a fissure in the hull.

Across the lagoon, the makeshift platform began to list. But Nose, Truman, and Elvira hadn't stopped cranking.

Sawyer wove through a maze of dim, funky tunnels. Overhead, daylight stabbed through seams in the deck. Nearby, another shiny object beckoned from a jumble of debris.

22

FOREVER IN BLOOM

OL' ONE EYE WAS GROWING TIRED. HIS LEAPS HAD BECOME more desperate than spectacular. His movements were sluggish.

"We're winning! He's wearing out!" yelled Truman.

Elvira was in tears. "He's dead, isn't he? Sawyer's dead," she repeated over and over as she struggled at the winch.

"Keep pullin', Vi," Nose shouted. "We gotta reel him in!"

"I don't care anymore," she moaned. "I just want my brother."

"We can't give up," said Truman. "Not now. We can do this. We *gotta* do this—for Sawyer."

"For Sawyer!" chimed Nose.

"For Sawyer," said Elvira miserably.

Now, a fourth pair of hands reached in from behind. "Yeah, do it for me."

"Sawyer!" the others shouted.

The team redoubled their efforts. Ol' One Eye slowly plowed back and forth, circling the lagoon in ever diminishing loops.

"What's our time, Tru?" asked Nose.

Truman consulted his watch. "One hour, fifty-eight minutes, thirty-four seconds," he replied.

The sun climbed the cerulean sky, burning off the morning mist. Sawyer and Elvira cranked the winch while Nose and Truman rested. They had been working in shifts for the past hour, while Ol' One Eye rested and fought, rested and fought.

Time after time they hauled him close to the deck, winching laboriously crank by crank. And just when they thought he had struggled his last, the great fish would summon some fathomless reserve of strength and renew the fight. Each time, they had to release the winch and let out the line, or their precarious craft would sink. Then the wily beast would seem to play dead, while two pairs of aching, tired arms cranked him back toward the deck.

"What's our time, Tru?" Sawyer sighed.

"'Two hours, forty-eight minutes, nineteen seconds," reported Truman.

The sun shone directly overhead. The derrick was still intact, but the floating deck listed heavily. While one team winched, the other sat on the opposite side, balancing the weight.

Nose and Truman were at the winch. Sawyer watched Ol' One Eye, waiting for him to rear and bolt once more. Closer and closer they hauled the beast, and still he did not move. Ten yards. Nothing. Five yards. Nothing.

Sawyer sat up straight. "Look alive, team," he warned the others. Nose and Truman perked up. Elvira stared passively.

Three yards. Two. One.

At last, the mythic monster was alongside. He bobbed listlessly, his scarred and empty eye socket staring to the sky.

Sawyer and Elvira crossed to the winch. Four pairs of blistered hands, eight straining arms, four aching backs laid into the winch. Inch by inch, they raised their trophy from the water, every moment expecting the huge fish to begin thrashing wildly.

Foot after foot of glistening fish flesh emerged from the lagoon. They stopped winching and collapsed in a heap. Ol' One Eye was suspended in midair.

Nose brushed his fingertips against the cat's cool, silky flesh. He turned to Truman and was about to speak when the awesome fish gave a final twitch and twirl. Sawyer and Elvira stepped back. Truman ducked as the dorsal swung around. Nose was slow to react, and the resulting slap whacked him flush across the face.

It sounded like he'd been hit by a pillowcase filled with clammy Jell-O. Nose staggered and swayed like a punch-drunk prizefighter. The others tried to anticipate where he might drop and moved into position to break his fall. Naturally, he hit the deck in the other direction.

Nose lay still and vacant eyed. Sawyer cradled his head. Elvira tore away a pocket from her coveralls and dabbed at the blood seeping from his swelling nose. Truman checked his pulse.

"What's our time now, Tru?" Nose muttered groggily.

Sawyer and Elvira helped Nose to his feet while Truman checked his watch.

"Four hours, twenty-two minutes, thirty-three seconds."

It was early afternoon. The exhausted anglers sprawled on the listing deck. Ol' One Eye hung limp, like a broad white sail becalmed upon a yardarm.

Sawyer picked up the battered Barbie lunch box and shook it. The contents rattled. His companions looked up. Sawyer shook the box again, his face expressionless.

"What?" said Nose wearily.

Sawyer pushed the lunch box toward them.

"Barbie—?" said Elvira hopefully. But she had seen her poor Barbie disappear down Ol' One Eye's greedy gullet. She opened the lid, looked inside—and gasped! "You found it? You found the treasure!"

Elvira, Nose, and Truman reached in and began to sort through the curious contents: Assorted bottle caps and buttons, a corroded Confederate belt buckle, a warped harmonica, a rusty dog tag. A tarnished bracelet, some green-crusted coins. A pair of bent and cracked wire-rimmed spectacles, an ancient padlock, a broken compass. A silver thimble.

Sawyer watched his friends pick though the odds and ends. They were excited about his discovery, but he felt only sadness and disappointment. It seemed they'd found just about everything—everything except a ring. His shoulders slumped. Elvira scooted next to her brother and put her arm around him.

"What's this?" said Truman, hoping to distract them. He picked up an odd muddy lump. Sawyer shrugged. Truman swished it through the water. He examined it closely. "Well, I'll be!" he said.

"What?" said Elvira.

"A tooth," said Truman. "A gold tooth. That has to be worth something."

"Lemme see that," said Sawyer. He took the small object in his hand. Could this be Moses's missing tooth? But Sawyer was too tired and depressed to explain. He tossed the tooth back into the lunch box, then rose and stepped away from the others.

Nose picked up the bone-shaped tag. Rubbing at the rust, he made out an inscribed name. "Hub—Hubi—Hubbie! Holy Cow! My grandpa told me when he was a kid he had a dog named Hubbie. He's not gonna believe this."

"Thought you were running away from home once you caught Ol' One Eye," Truman reminded him.

Nose paused and then shook his head. "Nah. You

kidding? Moses was right. I got the Delta in me." He reached for the harmonica, but Truman was quicker.

Nose winced. "What do you think you're gonna do with that?" he asked.

"Hey, I'm a musician, right?" replied Truman.

He brought the waterlogged instrument to his lips and blew a brief, discordant wail. Nose made a face like his eardrums were bursting. Elvira clapped her hands over her ears. Truman shook the harmonica, spraying Nose with lagoon water. He filled his lungs and blew again. It sounded like he was tuning a bobcat. The unsettling note carried off across the water.

Sawyer stood apart, looking across the lagoon. He spoke softly to himself.

"Wherever," he began.

He hesitated, trying to remember.

"You say something, Saw?" asked Nose.

"Wherever you are . . ."

Another pause.

"Whatever you do . . ."

Sawyer turned to the motley crew looking back at him.

"Wherever we are, whatever we do, we'll always remember."

Nose and Truman exchanged a confused look.

"Nothing is lost."

The others stared back. They hadn't the faintest idea what Sawyer was going on about, but they could see it meant a lot to him.

"I know it's confusing. But will you remember it?" Sawyer asked.

The question hung like Ol' One Eye in the humid air.

"Whatever you say, Saw," replied Nose. He didn't know what else to add.

"Thanks for the tip," Truman said, equally tongue-tied.

Elvira stood and went to her brother. She wrapped her arms around his middle.

"What's wrong, Sawyer?" she asked.

"I saw Dad."

"Daddy? You saw Daddy? When? Where?"

"On the river."

"Can I see him, too? Let's go back!"

"He can't come with us. He's on a different river now."

"What river? Where?" She tugged at his arm. "We have to go back!"

"I don't know. But it's a long way from here, farther away than we can ever go. He said he has his river, and the Yazoo is mine now."

"What does that mean?"

"I think it means we're on our own." Sawyer's voice wavered. He sank to his knees and squeezed her tight. His eyes were wet.

Nose and Truman turned away. Truman fidgeted with the harmonica. He put it to his lips again, and blew. This time a round object shot from between the reeds and clattered across the deck. It rolled in circles until finally, it stopped.

Everyone held still. There was no mistake: it was a *ring*!

Sawyer scooped up the cracked spectacles and perched them on his nose. He picked up the ring and examined it. The magnified image bore an inscription. He read out loud: "To My Rose, Forever in Bloom."

Elvira gasped. "Rose? Sawyer—that's Mom's—"

Brother and sister locked eyes—and smiled.

"This just might be her miracle," Sawyer said, holding up the prize.

Sawyer removed the spectacles. "Let's go home."

23

DOWN THE YAZOO

AS NIGHTFALL CLOAKED THE BAYOU, FOUR SILHOUETTES push-poled a makeshift raft across the lost lagoon. The legendary leviathan was now laid out onboard, shrouded in tattered red velvet saloon drapes.

Elvira had been distraught that her baby stork was nowhere to be found. Sawyer assured her that the stork had returned to its parents. "And that's just what we need do," he'd said.

They pushed toward the channel that Sawyer had spotted from the pilothouse. Elvira plopped down next to Ol' One Eye and lay just as motionless, staring up at the darkening sky. The moon had not yet risen, and she could see the brightest stars beginning to shine.

"There's the Big Dipper," she said dreamily.

"And the North Star," added Truman. "See the two

stars on the outside of the Dipper's cup? They point right to Polaris."

Sawyer nodded. "Yep," he said, as they poled into the channel. "We're headed north."

"And north is home?" said Nose.

"I reckon so," said Sawyer.

It was the first time Nose had spoken since setting forth from the lagoon. After his smack in the sniffer from Ol' One Eye, he'd begun to experience the world in a way that he'd nearly forgotten. He sampled a stew of swampy aromas: the strong cedar-like perfume of cypress, the sweet scent of tupelo gum, the intoxicating spice of longleaf pine. Not all the smells were pleasant, but all were welcome. When he was ready to share his news, Grandpa Moses would be the first to know.

The poling was slow going. Elvira had dozed off, and the boys were almost too pooped to push. But eventually the *Delta Belle* was left behind and after rounding a bend, they could see her no more.

Tall cypresses closed over their heads, hiding the stars. But the channel seemed to run fairly straight, and they pushed on.

Before long, the rising three-quarter moon flickered through the treetops. The sky was opening up just ahead, as the channel joined a broader expanse of flowing water. The boys turned their craft downstream.

The going was easier now, with the current in their favor. The air was less close, and a cool breeze soothed their

FISHTALE

aching bodies. The pulsing rhythms of countless crickets lulled them nearly to sleep. The moon shone brightly, reflected on the water.

Truman, poling halfheartedly, noticed a yellow shape in the moonlight along the starboard side. "Is that what I think it is?" he said.

Sawyer and Nose nodded.

"I knew it," breathed Sawyer.

"We're down the Yazoo," whispered Nose.

They drifted past the familiar landmarks from Moses's lost map—the sunken school bus, the lightning tree, the broken bridge.

A distant cluster of twinkling lights appeared on the riverbank. Soon the dark outline of their town took shape. Weary but triumphant, they poled the final distance to the Main Street Pier. Sawyer nudged his sister. She sat up, rubbing her eyes.

"We made it," she murmured.

The streets were empty. The town was shut down tighter than a clamshell. A lone traffic light flashed caution.

Sawyer was first to climb to the pier. "I gotta get home," he said.

"Me, too," said Elvira.

"No way, Vi. You stay here."

"Why?"

"Because you can't. You just can't."

"She's my mother, too," Elvira protested.

Sawyer placed a hand on her shoulder and bent close.

"You're the one who first hooked Ol' One Eye, aren't you?"

Elvira looked to Nose and Truman. They nodded, and she beamed with pride.

"Well, uh, yeah. I guess I am."

"Then he's your responsibility. You gotta make sure no one steals him. You gotta get him to the town scale to make it official."

He was referring to the oversized scale for weighing fish standing vigil up the street in the dark town square. It was more a monument and a symbol of their local culture, but it was still a working scale. There was a decent scale right there on the pier for weighing a good-sized catch, but no one had ever caught anything near the size of Ol' One Eye.

Nose and Truman turned to the beached behemoth. When they turned back, Sawyer was already sprinting up the street.

"How're we gonna get my fish all the way up there so we can weigh him?" Elvira asked.

Truman gave the problem some consideration, then gestured to a parked truck loaded with lengths of slender metal pipe. "You guys ever watch *The Ten Commandments* on TV?"

"Our mom made us watch." Elvira shrugged.

"Our TV don't work," said Nose.

"Doesn't matter," said Truman. "I'm going to show you how those pharaohs built their pyramids."

• • •

The town's few lights were now far behind. The first cat pond came within view, followed by another and another. Sawyer ran along the levees beside a dozen moons reflected on the surface of a dozen ponds.

He slowed to a trot. Before him lay the brood pond guarded by the scarecrow tending a flock of spectral cormorants. Their ringleader perched atop the tin pail head. Sawyer had never feared the birds before, but now their presence seemed menacing. He took a tentative step, shooing them with his arms, but they held their ground.

"Get lost, scram, beat it!" he shouted, half pleading, half demanding, but they refused to budge. He took off a sneaker and threw it. The birds responded only with their raspy grunts.

Sawyer had no choice but to pass among them. Their gray feathery shapes brushed against him. He paused to retrieve his sneaker. A bird pecked at his pocket containing the ring, and he swatted it away.

He ran on.

Ahead lay the Brown farm, the porchlight still on at this late hour. Sawyer froze. He recognized the car parked by the porch steps. The screen door opened and Doc Marsh emerged, carrying his doctor's bag. He climbed into the car and drove off.

What was Doc Marsh doing here so late? It must've

been nearly midnight. Sawyer forced himself to approach the house.

Back on Belzoni's main street, if you just happened to be a light sleeper and had ventured out for a midnight stroll, you'd have come upon an unusual sight—Ol' One Eye, laid out on a platform of pipes, with chains and ropes tied around his thick neck, and three very tired, straining children, dragging that velvet-shrouded beast.

POP! Truman's rope snapped and he pitched forward. Ol' One Eye began rolling backward, scattering pipes as he went. Nose and Elvira dug in their heels. Nose's rope snapped and sent him sprawling. Elvira tightened her grip. The rolling catfish dragged her down the street, toward the river. She had to let go.

Ol' One Eye hydroplaned in the dirt and made a complete about-face, his bullet head pointing back to the river.

Elvira picked herself up and knelt beside their catch. She drew the velvet shroud aside. She was eyeball-to-eyeball with Ol' One Eye. "I'm sorry if we hurt you," she whispered.

The leviathan's good eye opened and closed. Elvira yelped and leapt to her feet.

She pointed a shaky hand at the fish. "He—he winked."

Nose and Truman shuddered, then immediately armed themselves with metal pipes. Nose shuffled forward and nudged the catfish with his pipe, then retreated. There was no reaction from the fish.

"Just 'cause you're crazy doesn't give you the right to drive us nuts, Elvira," said Nose.

"Besides," said Truman, "fish can't wink. They don't have eyelids."

"Trust me," Elvira said. "He winked."

Sawyer entered the house. He made his way through silent rooms to the rear porch where his mother often slept on warm summer nights. The light was dim, but there was enough to see that the daybed was empty.

He climbed the stairs to her bedroom, knocked, and entered. It was dark inside. He turned on a light. Her bed was neatly made and clearly hadn't been slept in.

Returning downstairs, he saw a band of light coming from under the kitchen door. He poked his head in. She stood before the stove, dressed in her favorite bathrobe, frying something.

"Mom—?"

Mrs. Brown turned and her face lit up. "Sawyer!" She put down her spatula and gave him a bear hug.

"I didn't expect you to be gone so long! We were worried. Your Aunt Sarah's 'bout fit to be tied! We were going to call the sheriff in the morning," she said.

"Sorry," said Sawyer. "It took longer than I thought—"

"Well, goodness. What happened? You look like you fell off a cliff and landed in a bramble bush!"

She turned him around and gazed upon him head to foot.

"I'm okay, Mom. Really, I am."

"Where's your sister?"

"She's with Ol'—ah, with Truman and Nose."

"Where?"

"Down at the dock."

Mrs. Brown frowned. "I think it's time to be getting her home, don't you?"

"I'll go get her," said Sawyer. "So—what're you doing up so late?"

"Waiting for you and your sister, young man. That and a sudden craving for hush puppies. Imagine that. You hungry?"

"Starved," said Sawyer, eyeing the pan.

"Well—" said Mrs. Brown. "Did you catch anything?"

Sawyer reached into his pocket. "Sure did," he said. "Mom—how are you?"

"I feel a whole lot better, Sawyer, and the new test results say I've improved. Doc Marsh came to give me a shot, but I don't think I really needed it."

"I knew it! I knew it!"

"You knew what?" asked Mrs. Brown.

"I knew you'd be better."

"And how did you know that, sweetheart?"

Sawyer came close and extended a clenched fist. Opening his palm, he revealed the small gold band.

"Sawyer—?" She took the ring and studied it in the

kitchen light. Silently she read the inscription. Tears sprang to her eyes. "How did you—?"

"I think I'll let Elvira tell it," he said.

"Oh, Sawyer, honey—seems I've got the best medicine in the world right here." She embraced her son again. "There's nobody in this whole world who feels better than me right now."

"You really mean it?"

She slipped the ring on her finger. Her smile made her face glow. "Thanks for taking care of your sister this weekend. I know you weren't planning to have her along."

"It's okay," said Sawyer.

"She left me a note." Mrs. Brown handed him a sheet of folded paper from her pocket.

A crayon spelled out the word "GONE," followed by a crude drawing of a catfish, followed by the letters "ING." It was signed—"LOVE, ELVIRA."

Sawyer laughed.

"You know how thorough she is," said Mrs. Brown.

"Mom, I'll be back soon, okay?" he said.

"Where're you off to now?"

"I just gotta do something."

"I'll drive you."

"No, Mom, we started something, and now we have to finish."

Mrs. Brown hesitated

"You'll see," Sawyer assured her.

"Sawyer—"

"Yes?"

"I think your dad would be real proud of you." Mrs. Brown rested her hand on Sawyer's shoulder.

"Thanks, Mom," he said softly. He turned away. "Be back soon," he called as he bolted toward the stairs. He ran up to his bedroom and rummaged in a dresser drawer until he found his Polaroid camera.

The porch door banged open and he bounded down the steps, sprinting back between the cat ponds; this time, the cormorants scattered as he flew by.

It wasn't long before he saw a shower of bright sparks. Moses was out in his yard, wielding a blowtorch, working on his catfish sculpture.

"Moses!" he shouted.

Moses turned off the torch and raised his welder's mask. "Sawyer! You're back! You seen your mom?"

"Yeah!" He closed the distance and threw himself into Moses's arms.

"You were right, Moses. Anything's possible in Catfish Time."

Moses hugged him back. "Toldja."

Sawyer broke the embrace and fished in his pocket. He opened his palm.

"What's this?" asked the old man.

"Oh, nothing," said Sawyer. "Nothing but a gold tooth!"

"What?" exclaimed Moses, taking the tooth. "Well, my oh my! What *have* you whippersnappers been up to?"

"We caught him, Moses! Just like you said, only about ten times bigger. He'll make your eyes pop!"

Moses stared at Sawyer. "Slow down, son. What're you talkin' about?"

"*Ol' One Eye!* C'mon. We're gonna need help weighing him."

"Ol' One Eye? Get outta here." Moses turned back to his sculpture.

"What's the matter, Moses? You don't believe no more? Guess you're just too old to feel the power."

The old man opened his hand and looked at the gold tooth. A slow grin spread across his face.

"I think I'm beginnin' to feel it, Sawyer. Lead the way!"

24

MAIN STREET PIER

Nose, Truman, and Elvira were sprawled on their backs, their heads propped against Ol' One Eye like the world's biggest, puffiest pillow.

Nose studied Hubbie's dog tag. Truman blew a mournful tune on the harmonica. Elvira rolled over on her stomach and winked at Ol' One Eye, hoping for another wink in return. But the fish lay still.

Twin headlights flashed at the far end of the street and advanced in their direction. They climbed to their feet as Moses's station wagon rolled to a stop.

The door opened, and Sawyer ran toward them. Moses was right behind. His eyes wide in disbelief, the old man circled the velvet-shrouded prize.

Elvira looked anxiously at her brother.

"Mom's gonna be okay," Sawyer reassured her. "She's gonna be around for a long, long time."

Elvira threw her arms around him, squeezing him as hard as she could. He hugged her back till she had to pry him loose.

Nose embraced his grandfather. "Whatcha think, Gramps?"

Moses drew Nose close. "What do I think? I think I ought to steal you from your folks and keep you around forever. That's what I think."

Nose grinned.

"Also think we're gonna need us a tow truck. And the filling station doesn't open till dawn," Moses added.

Sawyer handed Moses his camera. "Can you take our picture?"

"Be my honor," he said.

The four fishermen lined up behind Ol' One Eye.

"Spread your arms," called Moses.

They moved apart and spread their arms wide, fingertips barely touching. Ol' One Eye was still longer than they were.

Click. The camera flashed.

"That's the last one," said Moses, checking the film. He returned to the station wagon and brought out a sack containing a loaf of bread, a package of bologna, and a six pack of Yoo-hoos.

Moses had never seen a loaf of bread disappear so fast.

The fishermen all felt certain they'd never tasted anything as good as a bologna sandwich.

As they finished their meal, exhaustion began to take its toll. Eyelids drooped. Heads nodded.

Minutes later, they'd settled into the station wagon to wait for Belzoni to wake. Moses and Nose were in the front seat, Truman had the backseat to himself, and Sawyer and Elvira made themselves comfortable in the cargo bed.

Half-waking dreams began to haunt Sawyer. Murky water, sunken boilers, once-shiny objects gone to rust, a massive albino beast walking on its fins, a humongous thrashing fishtail. He jerked awake. Was he dreaming? Or had he heard—

Sawyer struggled to lift his tired head. He glimpsed the silhouette of that fantastic fish, lying still, cloaked in regal red velvet.

Sawyer lay back. Overhead, lightning bugs glimmered and flitted among the stars. From up the street he heard the town's clock tower strike midnight.

"The miracle of Catfish Time," whispered Sawyer. He closed his eyes.

Dawn crept into the nooks and crannies of the Mississippi Delta town. Moses and Nose snored in harmony. Truman and Elvira lay deep in slumber. A rooster crowed in the distance.

Sawyer stirred. He rubbed the sleep from his eyes.

Climbing out of the car and standing in the empty street,

he felt a rush of alarm. Something was terribly wrong! He bent to the piece of red velvet bundled on the ground.

Ol' One Eye was gone!

Beyond the scraps of fabric, he came across Elvira's Barbie, coated in a sheen of glistening glop. Farther on lay a misshapen accordion in a pool of viscous slime. A small crab crawled from a tear in the bellows. Ahead lay another scrap of velvet.

Looking across the town green to the Yazoo, Sawyer made out a pattern of gouges littered with red velvet, weaving all the way to the riverbank.

One by one, the others woke. They joined Sawyer, staring toward the river.

Elvira wiped off the doll with the hem of her shirt. Truman inspected his battered accordion. Nose nudged a shred of velvet with his toe. There was no need to speak.

They all walked to the pier and stared down at the water. Their reflections stared back at them.

"I told you he winked," Elvira said.

Their gazes followed the wide expanse of the Yazoo. Somewhere out there was one heck of a big fish.

The Catfish King.

25

FISHTALE

"FROM TIME TO TIME WE STILL HEAR OF SIGHTINGS, BUT nothing's ever come of them. . . ." said Elvira.

She'd finished. The tale had been told yet again.

It was past closing time at the World Catfish Museum. Outside, afternoon had turned to evening. Inside, a clock ticked softly. General Leigh sighed and twitched in her sleep. Bernie sat in the gathering shadows, looking at Elvira. She could pretty much guess his thoughts.

"Once in a while, somebody's hunting dog'll go missing, and I'll get to wondering if Ol' One Eye's back in the neighborhood," Elvira said, to fill the silence.

"And your brother? Is he still around?"

"Sawyer took over running the family farm," she said. "Think he's got about a thousand acres underwater. Biggest cat farm in the state. Back when our mom was running it, we were just getting by. Now cat farming's big business. I expect we might run into him later. He's married, has a couple of kids, a boy and a girl."

"And your mother?"

"Thirteen years later, the leukemia caught up with her. She died the year I graduated from Mississippi State. She saw us through our growin' up years. That's what really matters."

"And your friends? Where are they now?" Bernie asked.

"You saw that cat sculpture out front?"

"Be kind of hard to miss," Bernie noted.

"Well, that's one of Moses's. He retired from the plant, but still makes his sculptures. Waldo did some traveling and settled down over in Louisiana. He's a ranger with the Department of Fish and Game. Hunts poachers for a living. It's dangerous work, but he's got a nose for it."

Bernie smiled.

"We saw a lot of Truman after that year. He spent nearly every summer with us. He calls from time to time. He gave up the accordion and took up the bass. Plays with a big-time blues band."

Elvira switched on a desk lamp. She fingered a golden ring dangling from a thong around her neck.

Bernie leaned forward. "Is that it?"

"Sure is," she said. "It passed on to me."

Bernie settled back again. "Well, I've got to hand it to you. That's quite a story."

"Question is, you buy any of it?"

Bernie chuckled. "No offense, but part of me's still wondering if you're pulling this Yankee's leg."

"None taken," she said, and meant it.

"Same old story though, huh?"

"What's that?" Elvira asked.

"The one that got away. A fishtale."

"There *is* one more thing," she said.

Elvira reached under her desk and dialed the combination on a small safe. General Leigh woke up and stretched. Elvira removed a swatch of red fabric. Wrapped inside was an envelope, from which she took a dog-eared photograph. She reached across the desk and handed it to Bernie.

He examined the photo. He turned it upside down, looked at it some more. He looked at it from every possible angle.

"Could be just about anything," he said at last.

"Could be," Elvira agreed.

He handed it back.

She placed the photo on the miniature scales she kept as a paperweight.

"So, you in the mood for some catfish pie?" she asked.

"I'll give it a try," Bernie replied.

And with that, they rose and stretched and stepped into the perfect evening to join the festival.

Elvira had told her tale for what must have been the trillionth time. Odds were tomorrow she might have to tell it again. And why not? It *was* one heck of a fishtale.

. . .

General Leigh remained behind in the cool office. A fly buzzed around the glass display case. The shelves, lined with faded red velvet, displayed a warped harmonica, cracked spectacles, a rusty dog tag, a silver thimble, a broken compass, a tarnished bracelet, an ancient padlock, and assorted odds and ends.

On Elvira's desk, the faded Polaroid—taken on a warm summer night many years before—balanced atop the miniature scales. And then, those scales tipped, just a smidge. General Leigh cocked her head.

To that day, it was the closest anyone had ever come to weighing that mighty fish.

In the photo, four pairs of scrawny legs, bruised, scratched, scabbed, and chigger bit, stood behind a torpedo-sized, velvet-shrouded shape on a dark, small-town Mississippi street.

GONE ING

LOVE, ELVIRA